A Dinah Galloway Mystery

The Man in the Moonstone

MELANIE JACKSON

ORCA BOOK PUBLISHERS

National Library of Canada Cataloguing in Publication Data
Jackson, Melanie, 1956-

The man in the moonstone / Melanie Jackson.

"A Dinah Galloway Mystery".

ISBN 1-55143-264-1

I. Title.

PS8569.A265M36 2003   jC813'.6   C2002-911535-3

PZ7. J1366Ma 2003

First published in the United States, 2003

Library of Congress Control Number: 2002117134

Summary: When Dinah gets a part in the musical adaptation of Wilkie Collins' *The Moonstone*, she stumbles onto a plot to steal a priceless ring.

Orca Book Publishers gratefully acknowledges the support for its publishing programs provided by the following agencies: the Government of Canada through the Book Publishing Industry Development Program (BPIDP), the Canada Council for the Arts, and the British Columbia Arts Council.

Cover design: Christine Toller
Cover illustration: Rose Cowles
Printed and bound in Canada

05 04 03 • 5 4 3 2 1

IN CANADA:
Orca Book Publishers
1030 North Park Street
Victoria, BC Canada
V8T 1C6

IN THE UNITED STATES:
Orca Book Publishers
PO Box 468
Custer, WA USA
98240-0468

To Pearl Chandler and Esther Galloway,
and the memories of Iowa
MJ

My Usual Dinah-Mite Intro

The moonstone was a ring. A shimmer of white or silver, or just shadows, depending how the light fell on it.

The moonstone was also the cause of a lot of trouble, as you're about to find out.

But there's another moonstone. It's a novel, *The Moonstone* (well, duh), by Wilkie Collins, published in 1868. And you know what? It was the first mystery ever to feature a detective.

People tend to forget that, because of the much more famous detective who came along later. You know the one.

... WHAT? No, *not* Sherlock Holmes!

Me.

As in,

Yours truly,
DINAH GALLOWAY

1.
The mysterious beak-nose

His face was large, round and pale. Kind of sad-looking, I thought. Maybe because this October night was cold, and he was all alone.

I nudged my sister, who was flipping through a fashion magazine. Specifically, a fashion magazine on prom dresses: she would be graduating at the end of this school year. "Hey, Madge, he's winking!"

Madge was busy examining a dress that, to my eleven-year-old eyes, looked like it was held up by two strands of dental floss. She shrugged me off. "It's just some idiot. Ignore him."

With her dark red hair, vivid blue eyes and creamy skin, Madge was used to being winked at. And gawked at. Once in a while a particularly stunned male would collide with a tree or telephone pole. Honest. Madge had a dreamy delicate aloofness that transformed men into, as she said, idiots.

"No-o-o-o." In saying this, I expelled a long trail of steam that charged down the line of people ahead of us. "Not some idiot. The *moon*, Madge."

She looked up. There the moon floated, silvery and fat, above the Livingston Theater. It spilled a wan light onto Vancouver's Granville Street; onto us hopefuls waiting to audition for a play; onto my glasses, which I'd just taken off to rub clean.

Two reflected moons glimmered at me from the lenses. "You see?" Madge said, smiling. "Most of us wish for the moon, but you've already got it. Twice over."

"Not the moon." A tall, beak-nosed woman with a bird's nest of black hair crammed into a bun was frowning at Madge and me. She was also pursing her lips in disgust at the still hovering cloud of steam I'd sent out, as if it had rudely invaded her personal space.

"*The Moonstone*," she continued crossly. "A musical version of the classic mystery by Wilkie Collins."

She sniffed, as if Madge and I were far too lowly to understand a "classic." In fact, we'd looked up *The Moonstone* on the Internet that afternoon. The story's about a huge gem that gets smuggled from India to England, where it's presented to a young bride-to-be, Rachel Verinder, as a wedding gift.

Problem is, the moonstone is full of curses as well as carats. Horrible things start happening to Rachel. The gem is stolen — with her fiancé the number one suspect.

"Hmph!" commented the beak-nosed woman. "Obviously they're letting *anyone* audition. Very democratic of them, I suppose."

"We're not 'anyone,' " Madge returned pleasantly. "My sister is Dinah Galloway. The talented Dinah Galloway, I should say. If you haven't heard *of* her, you've probably heard her. Dinah's sung on a couple of radio commercials."

"I was the Singing Salami," I chipped in, wondering why the woman's face was growing even more pinched. "You know, for Sol's Salami, on West Fourth."

"And what part would a — a Singing Salami be trying out for in *The Moonstone?*"

"Coretta Cuff," I said promptly. "My agent, Mr. Wellman, suggested it."

Mr. Wellman had explained to me that the producers of this *Moonstone* play were lightening it up from the novel, which wasn't exactly a laugh fest. Besides turning the story into a musical, they'd changed the character of the detective. In the novel, a dour Sergeant Cuff solves the mystery of the missing moonstone. In this play, the sleuth would be an amateur one, a girl, *Coretta* Cuff.

Coretta was a houseguest who happened to have strong sleuthing abilities — and, this version being a musical one, strong singing abilities, as well.

Anyhow, the changes, Mr. Wellman had said, were to make the play more appealing to a modern audience.

Beak-Nose ran a haughty gaze over me. Clearly she did not think a chubby pre-teen with untidy reddish brown hair and smudged glasses would appeal to anyone.

In an effort to look more respectable, I smoothed down my bangs and stared back at her. "What are *you* auditioning for?" I demanded. I tried to remember the different parts in the script Mr. Wellman had given me. "Oh-h-h ... are you the friend of Rachel who gets hacked up?"

The woman's features pursed so tightly that the nostrils on her beaked nose closed up altogether. "I should say not!" she replied, in a choked voice. "I am Mrs. Violet Bridey, with enough experience in theater" — she pronounced it *theatah* — "that I would hardly agree to be 'hacked up,' as you crudely put it. My niece Angela is the one trying out. For the role of Coretta Cuff," she added, with yet another sniff.

Curving one black-gloved hand like a fishhook, she reached down and plucked a girl about my age from beside her. She spun the girl round by the shoulder to face us. "My *accomplished* niece, Angela Bridey," the woman said, with a trembling, scornful smile. "Naturally, when Angela gets the part of Coretta, I shall be with her at every rehearsal, coaching and advising nonstop."

Angela Bridey was long and thin, like her aunt, with a thick dramatic black mane of hair that contrasted startlingly with her pale skin. In the white moonlight, she blinked uncertainly at us. I wondered how Angela really felt about the prospect of all this nonstop coaching and advising.

I was also thinking: This kid is too scared and pinched-looking to be Coretta Cuff. Coretta was supposed to be feisty! Also wacky and funny.

Feisty ... wacky ... funny ... That was me, Dinah Galloway, all over.

Nope, this pale kid wouldn't be right at all. She just couldn't get the part.

Could she?

"Hi, Angela," said Madge, because I was too busy staring.

Beak-Nose Bridey squeezed that fishhook-like hand on Angela's shoulder. "Young Angela," she informed us, "comes here with *Ross*."

I didn't see any Ross around. That is, aunt and niece appeared to be on their own. I brightened. "Hey! Is Ross your pet rat or something? Where is he, in your pocket?"

Madge held up her fashion magazine to cover a peculiar-sounding cough.

Beak-Nose stiffened. "Not Ross. R.O.S.," she spelled out. "Angela has taken years of classical Royal Opera Society training. She has her R.O.S. certificate. Give them a high C, Angela," Beak-Nose commanded. "Go on."

The obedient Angela dropped her lower lip. A pure, ringing operatic note shot out, silencing the chatter of other auditioners up and down the line. When the last echo of the note had faded, several people applauded.

Including me. "No way I could sing like that," I said truthfully.

"That was excellent, Angela," Madge said, but she was regarding Angela's aunt icily.

Older sisters are weird. They feel total license to be ultra critical and snooty with you themselves. But let someone else be rude to you, and wow! Suddenly they're fierce avengers. A very peculiar breed.

"Dinah, dear," Madge said, not removing her glacial gaze from Beak-Nose, "why don't you give us a middle C?"

Dinah *dear*? I gaped at Madge, wondering if the October chill had got to her brain.

Then I happened to look at Beak-Nose. She was gaping at *me* — and here's the funny thing I then realized about moonlight. Being stark and luminous, it kind of double-exposes people, like a film negative. Just for an instant I saw more in Beak-Nose's face than I was supposed to.

I saw — fear.

Huh? I thought. I hardly considered myself frightening. Unless Beak-Nose had a phobia about freckles.

I opened my mouth. A weak, off-key middle C limped out.

Madge stared at me. Actually, at my mouth, the way you do at a ketchup bottle when you're sure something's in there, but nothing's coming out. "Are you all right, Dinah?"

I opened my mouth again. This time I released an even feebler middle C. More like a middle Z.

Beak-Nose smirked. "I'm sure you make an excellent Singing Salami," she chortled. She spun Angela round by the shoulder again, shoving her ahead in line. Angela did glance back at me curiously, as if I were a specimen that had escaped from one of those science lab jars they have at school.

Madge began fussing over me, worrying about laryngitis or even pneumonia, but I ignored her. I was much more interested in the call that Beak-Nose, turning away from Angela, then punched in on her cell phone.

Angela couldn't hear her now, but I could. At least, by straining my ears I could. Curiosity should always be indulged, in my opinion.

"No competition that I can see. Or hear," Beak-Nose corrected herself and gave a chuckle as dry as dead leaves at her joke. "Soon we'll be on the *inside*."

Of course you'll be inside, I thought, puzzled. That's where the *Moonstone* tryouts were being held. Inside the Livingston Theater.

What a strange way to talk about an audition, I mused, as Madge anxiously buttoned up my duffel coat buttons right to my chin. Next she removed her scarf and covered my head with it, tucking the edges into my coat collar. At this rate, I'd soon resemble a mummy.

But I wasn't concerned about that. I was wondering:

Why had Beak-Nose deliberately prevented Angela from overhearing her phone call? What was so secret about it?

2.
And the part goes to ...

A piercing scream shattered the calm of the theater.

Even those of us waiting at the back of the theater had to cover our ears. "I was relieved when they let us in," Madge muttered to me. "I didn't expect to be deafened once we got here."

"Again, please," the director, sitting midway back, called to the young woman onstage.

"AAAAAGGGHHHH!"

"Wait a minute," I said, as Madge clamped her hands over her ears a second time. "I'd know that scream anywhere. It's Cindi Kahn."

"Excellent. You'll be hearing from us," the director promised Cindi, whose huge, goggly eyes bulged out even more at his words.

"Oooo, thank you," she breathed.

"We, on the other hand, may not be able to hear anything again," the director joked. Everyone laughed.

Except Cindi, who, looking stunned at her success, scurried up the aisle, her long corkscrew ringlets bobbing up and down.

"Hey," I greeted her.

Cindi and I knew each other because we had the same agent, Mr. Wellman. She often practiced her screams in the Wellman Talent Co. office.

"Dinah! Hi, Madge!" Cindi ran over to us, glowing. "Isn't this exciting? I might actually get the part of Rachel Verinder!"

The character of Rachel did lots and lots of screaming.

"I'm confident you'll get the part," I told Cindi.

"Oooo, I hope so," she giggled, rolling her big eyes. "You must be here for the Coretta Cuff role. You'll dazzle 'em, Ms. Dinah-Mite."

Madge looked up from a photo of a form-fitting white dress that to me resembled an empty paper-towel roll. "I'm not sure Ms. Dinah-Mite should even be here," she confided. "Her voice has gone all raspy. Could be a cold. I should probably take her home and tuck her into bed under a mountain of comforters."

Cindi made tut-tutting noises. She drew her purple fake-fur coat around herself more tightly and shivered in sympathy with me. "They shouldn't have forced us to wait outside, even if the moonlight *was* pretty." She arched well-plucked eyebrows that themselves were like half-moons.

She gave a melodramatic sigh. "So exciting about the moonstone, isn't it?" Cindi asked me.

"Sure, it's a cool play."

"Not the play. The ring," she said, but then somebody hissed, "Sssh!" and silenced her. Angela Bridey was walking onstage.

Her voice rose, clear, wistful, delicate, from the stage. It lilted on flute-like notes up and up to the rafters of the Livingston Theater.

Blue moon, you saw me standing alone
without a dream in my heart
without a love of my own.

This was to be the signature tune of the show. Angela sang it beautifully. Her voice reminded me of silver, of something so pure and fine it ought to be put carefully away afterward in a jewelry box.

You heard me saying a prayer for
someone I really could care for.

When Angela finished, there was a kind of stunned silence around the theater. Then, vigorous clapping. "Exquisite," someone murmured. "A second Charlotte Church," agreed another. Beak-Nose, stepping out to join her niece onstage, preened.

Madge gave me a hug. "So, Di. Shall we just pack it in and go home?"

"Honey and lemon'll fix you up," Cindi assured me. "And there will always be other auditions."

The director called to Angela, "Very impressive! You'll be hearing from us, Miss Bridey."

Then he got up, checking his watch, and walked over to those of us lined up against the back. He was youngish middle-aged, I saw, with gray-flecked brown hair and beard, and shrewd, thoughtful brown eyes behind round gold glasses. "Do we have any more Coretta Cuffs to audition?" he asked, with a questioning glance down at a woman who stood beside him. His assistant, I guessed.

"Um," said the woman, holding up a list of names attached to a clipboard. "There's one more. A Dinah Galloway." She brought the clipboard closer to her eyes to squint at the writing. "I don't understand: she has a singing salami?"

"It's okay," Madge said. "Dinah's not feeling that well, so I'm going to — "

I marched forward, out of Madge's hug and up to the edge of the stage. "I'll try out now," I announced.

I'd forgotten how thoroughly Madge had

bundled me up. My glasses were the only thing about me that showed. Therefore my words came out muffled, and I could see the director looking at me oddly.

"This is a musical of *The Moonstone* we're auditioning for," he explained. "Not *The Mummy's Curse*."

"Very funny," I said through Madge's scarf.

I hoisted myself onto the stage. Other auditioners had gone up by the stage steps at the side, but I preferred the direct route.

The man who'd been playing the piano for each singer helped me up. He was quite fat and had a toothpick between his teeth. It waggled as he spoke. "What'll it be, some theme music from *Invasion of the Body Snatchers*?"

I unwound the scarf from my face, removed my hat, coat and mittens, and handed all these to him. "I hope the jokes in the play are better than yours."

Grinning, he dumped my stuff on a nearby chair, on top of a jacket already dumped there. A faded orange-and-green plaid jacket, that is. I guessed fashion wasn't a big concern of the piano man's.

Then he slid onto the piano bench and tinkled out a few warm-up notes of "Blue Moon."

The director gave a faint, bemused shrug and

sat down beside his assistant again.

Near him, hovering in the aisle, was Beak-Nose. A scornful half-smile bent her long, thin face sideways. Her eyes, meanwhile, had narrowed to matchsticks.

"Blue ... " I began. A bit of fluff from Madge's scarf had got into my mouth. The note wobbled and died.

I hesitated. In singing "Blue Moon," Coretta was homesick for her father, who'd stayed in India with his British army regiment. She was supposed to sound as if she were suffering from loneliness, as opposed to laryngitis.

There were stirrings in the line of people at the back. The director tapped his pen on the seat ahead of him. The piano man stopped tinkling and glanced over his shoulder at me.

"Dinah," said Madge anxiously.

I spat out the bit of fluff and adjusted my glasses. "I might try one more time," I said.

Piano Man switched his toothpick to the other side of his mouth. I guess he liked variety in his life. He started playing again.

I heaved a deep breath. I was imagining the rows of seats out there were a giant swimming pool that I had to dive into.

Instead I dived into the song.

Blue moon, you saw me standing alone
without a dream in my heart
without a love of my own ...

My voice didn't float, like Angela's. It charged. It barged. It invaded the rafters — and every corner and every floorboard of the theater as well. In fact, I pitched it beyond all these, right through the walls and out to the round, pale, moody moon, because he'd looked so lonely.

Blue moon, you knew just what I was there for ...

I don't know why I always had to sing loudly, but I did. I was able to. It was just this gift I had. A godsend, Mother called it.

I've had instructors who talked about a strong voice coming from the diaphragm. But I knew my singing came right out of my heart, since it made me happy. It cleared any bad things away, just like ... well, just like opening the bathroom window cleared away the smell of our cat Wilfred's litter.

Anyhow, you get my point. I loved to belt out songs.

Now I'm no longer alo-o-one!

My voice wasn't something to be tucked carefully in a jewelry box for safekeeping. My voice would burst the bands of any box that tried to hold it and send the box's top, bottom and sides flying. That wasn't a judgment on Angela's voice, which I'd truly found lovely. That's just how it was with mine.

I finished "Blue Moon" and realized, almost with surprise, that I was in this shadowy theater with a bunch of people listening. I really had been concentrating on the moon.

The echoes hadn't even had time to fade away before raucous applause and shrill whistling erupted from everyone. There was no polite interval like Angela had got.

"Whoa, sister!' exclaimed Piano Man, swinging round on his bench. He stomped his feet as well as clapping. In his enthusiasm he bit the toothpick clean in half; the broken-off part dropped to the floor.

A hand reached down for it, gave it back to him. The director had come to the edge of the stage and was smiling up at me. "You're incredible," he said. "How do you do that?"

So I gave him my theory about how singing was like opening a window to offset a bad smell. His assistant giggled, but the director nodded quite solemnly.

"I understand," he said. "By the way, my name's Jon Horowitz."

He stretched up his hand, and I shook it, and he kept smiling — which was pretty decent of him, considering that my palm was chocolate-sticky from some M&M's I'd been eating in the lineup.

"You're my Coretta Cuff," Jon said. He grinned. "Man! First Cindi, then you. Does Wellman Talent represent any *quiet* performers?"

Everyone laughed. Everyone, that is, except Beak-Nose Bridey. A fierce scowl had deepened her already long face into lightning-bolt length.

I smiled a smug, quiet little smile. I'd fooled her. I was always able to sing, underneath the moon on Granville Street, or on a stage, or anywhere. But with certain people, especially scornful ones, it was sometimes fun to pretend I couldn't — at first. Never underestimate the pleasure of springing surprises, I like to say.

Snatching her cell from her shoulder bag, Beak-Nose punched a single button and a moment later was jabbering away, as Angela looked on unhappily. "No," Beak-Nose fumed. "Things didn't work out. We're *not* in."

A *single* button. Redial? Beak-Nose must've phoned back the person she'd talked to before. The one she'd assured, "Soon we'll be on the inside."

Why phone again now? And, aside from Angela not getting the part of Coretta, what "things" hadn't worked out?

"Weird," I muttered.

"Weird?" asked Jon. He swung me down off the stage. "There's nothing weird about it, kid. You just happen to have a Mack truck's worth of talent, that's all."

Madge hurried up to hug me. "I'm so proud of you, Dinah! How exciting!"

I shrugged modestly, but I did feel pleased. I'd landed one of the lead roles in a musical!

Angela Bridey may have had R.O.S.

I had V.O.L.U.M.E.

3.
Great-Uncle who?

"I'll tell you what Dinah does not have," said my principal.

There was a pause. Ms. Chen often created pauses, for effect. Outside the window, a dry red leaf floated down to brush against Lord Bithersby Elementary's faded peach brick wall.

Ms. Chen folded her hands on her desk and lifted her eyebrows at Mother, Jon and me. "Satisfactory marks in math," she finished.

I opened my mouth to object. It stayed open for a few moments before I thought of an actual objection. "I can explain the poor mark on this week's test," I blurted out at last. "It's the trauma of starting grade seven."

Ms. Chen's eyebrows rose a notch higher. "*You* aren't traumatized by anything. Which can be a problem, Dinah Galloway. Sometimes it's better to stop and reflect about things."

" 'Be bold, but not too bold,' " Mother quoted dreamily.

Jon looked at her — really looked at her — for the first time since the three of us had met in the Lord Bithersby parking lot to face down Ms. Chen.

Mother *was* dreamy, like Madge. She resembled Madge, too: a middle-aged, softened version. Softened like in late afternoon, when the sun slants low, with a kind of wistful light.

"Spenser. *The Faerie Queen*," Jon murmured. "Wow, Mrs. Galloway. That's very literary of you — and especially in a discussion about math."

"Oh, Mother's always quoting stuff," I informed him, delighted that the subject had veered away from my marks. "She loves books. Since Dad died she's been studying to be a librarian. She graduates this spring.

"So," I said, standing, "I guess that wraps up our discussion. Well! Gotta get to math class now. We're doing fractions. Mmm-mmm!" I exclaimed with hearty enthusiasm and started towards the door.

"JUST A MINUTE, DINAH." Ms. Chen didn't shout this, but she spoke in a deadly quiet tone that was as powerful as shouting. It's a strange, twisted gift that principals have. I sat down abruptly.

"As a matter of fact, your class *is* tackling fractions this week," Ms. Chen continued, in that same quiet tone. "Your being unable to distinguish between numerators and denominators is a strong argument against taking on this play."

"Oh, math schmath," I said impatiently. "What's it good for? I intend to be a singer or a detective, or maybe both. No need for numbers."

With his forefinger, Jon made a slitting motion across his throat. "*Cut*, Dinah. Bad attitude. You've just about argued yourself out of *The Moonstone*. Math is valuable, okay, kid? For example, to stage this play. Y'know, to position everybody in relation to the scenery and the audience. I'll have to think about angles and distances. *I'll have to use math*."

I won't though, I thought. I'm there to sing. And it's notes that come out, not numerators and denominators.

Still, I saw his point about adopting the right attitude with Ms. Chen. I scrunched my face up in my best effort to appear interested.

The principal snorted at me, which I found quite rude. After all, I *might* have been sincere. "Mr. Horowitz," she said. "Being in your play requires Dinah to be away from school a lot." She examined the government form for child labor that Mother and he had submitted. Being underage, I needed my principal's consent to work.

"Time when Dinah could be doing remedial work in math, which she so badly needs," added Ms. Chen.

I could feel my scrunched-up features beginning to sag. Ms. Chen couldn't, she just couldn't, refuse to sign the form!

Ms. Chen permitted herself the glimmer of a smile at me. "In language arts I have no worry at all. You express yourself very clearly, Dinah. That story you wrote, *The Spy in the Alley*, was vivid and colorful."

"Excuse me, Ms. Chen, but that wasn't a story," I objected. "It was a case. All true. You see, I stumbled on, or really it was my cat who stumbled on, this guy hiding in the bluebells and blackberries beside our back gate. It turns out he was — "

"Now, Dinah," Mother interrupted. "I'm sure we should keep to the subject at hand: math." She glanced apologetically from Ms. Chen to Jon. "My daughter is highly imaginative, as you see. The case — I mean story — Dinah refers to did happen. Though I can't believe I use the term 'godsend' as much as you claim I do," she told me.

Ms. Chen looked mildly frustrated; I beamed. In her dotty way, Mother had wandered far, far from the subject at hand.

Jon was gazing at Mother in fascination. "Maybe

you yourself are a godsend, Suzanne," he said quietly.

He hadn't called Mother by her first name before. On the phone, and meeting in person in the parking lot just now, he'd addressed her as "Mrs. Galloway." I myself didn't think of her as *Suzanne*. She was Mother, or, with her friends, Sue. There really was no Suzanne, I thought, as Mother, appearing quite surprised, blushed.

Suzanne was the name of a girl in some dumb romantic poem our substitute teacher, Mr. Paigely, had read to our class. (Our regular teacher, Ms. LaFontaine, off on sick leave, would never have done anything so silly.) Nobody had understood the poem, except for the words "her perfect body," which had made us giggle.

Girls in romantic poems ... No, the name Suzanne was hardly appropriate for my mother. I mean, my *mother*, for God's sake.

I was about to helpfully correct Jon on this point when he turned to Ms. Chen. "I could give Dinah remedial help in math," he offered, "during breaks in rehearsal. Or when my assistant director takes over for me."

"Um, Jon," I said, appalled. The point of being in a play during the school year was to miss lessons, not practice them.

"I was pretty good at math in high school,"

Jon went on, ignoring me. "And I am committed to the idea of kids getting a strong education — wherever they happen to be. I'm serious. I'm quite willing to keep Dinah up with the curriculum; even move her ahead a bit."

I made a gagging noise. "My breath is growing short," I informed them. "I may require medical attention."

"You'll live," Ms. Chen told me unsympathetically. She nodded to Jon. "Very well. You and I will talk to Dinah's teacher and see what we can work out."

Lifting a pen, she signed the consent form. Lifting a forefinger, I made the throat-slitting gesture at Jon.

But he didn't notice. He was busy smiling at Mother ...

My friend Pantelli Audia and I were shooting elastics at the substitute teacher's back when Ms. Chen appeared at the classroom door. Unlucky timing for Pantelli. He'd just fired an elastic. Over kids' heads it soared, bouncing off Mr. Paigely's back and ricocheting against his desk. The neat thing was, Mr. Paigely, busy writing numbers on the blackboard, hadn't felt any of our elastics.

"PANTELLI. MY OFFICE." That weird quiet

shouting again by Ms. Chen. Scratching his black, curly hair ruefully, Pantelli trotted off as I slid our bag of elastics into my lap.

"Phone call for you, Dinah," said Ms. Chen. "Your uncle, calling long distance. Sorry to interrupt, Mr. Paigely."

The substitute, in his first year and very nervous and eager to please — in other words, the type you would naturally aim elastics at — bobbed his head like a jack-in-the-box. "Oh, absolutely, Ms. Chen. No problem. Interrupt the class any time," he assured her.

Realizing he'd been waving his piece of chalk while he spoke, Mr. Paigely hastily set it down on his desk — only to notice a mountain of elastics piled on the blotting pad. "Uh ... "

"Yes, 'uh' indeed," Ms. Chen said dryly.

"Dinah, m'dear!" boomed a hearty voice in my ear. "It's Uncle Leo! Remember me?"

"Not exactly," I replied, holding the phone slightly away from my ear.

"Well, well, well!" he laughed. "Truth be told, I'm your great-uncle. Your dad's uncle: so sorry to hear about him, by the way. He was much too young to die."

There was a honking as Great-Uncle Leo blew his nose. With morbid interest I peered round from the school secretary's desk, where I was standing, into the principal's office.

Ms. Chen was telling off Pantelli. I caught fragments: " ... as one of the older students at Lord Bithersby, you should be more responsible ... " and "Mr. Paigely, trying so hard ... "

"A shame, a real shame," Great-Uncle Leo was saying. "When I heard about it, I said to m'self, 'Ain't that a kick in the head!' "

Another honking. I held the receiver even farther away.

"Hear you're goin' to be in a play," Leo declared. "What's it called — *The Millstone?*"

"*The Moonstone,*" I corrected. Boy, were there ever some eccentrics on Dad's side of the family!

Meanwhile I was still craning to see what was happening in the principal's office. Ms. Chen spotted me; hastily I backed out of her view.

Leo shouted, "A play! Ain't that a kick in the head! Contract not signed yet, though, is it? I mean, yer not in yet, are ya?"

"No-o-o," I replied slowly, wondering what this last remark of his reminded me of. Something someone had said. But who, and what? "My agent has to bring the contract round for us to sign."

"M'dear, tell ya what. For yer own good. DON'T sign."

"Huh? I don't — "

Leo's hearty voice turned dark and nasty, like a pit of tar. "Wouldn't want any harm to come to you, toots. It's a dangerous part, ya know what I mean? *Don't play Coretta*. Won't be good for yer health."

"But why? What do you mean?" I asked.

His voice returned to its former loud heartiness. "Just want the best for ya, dontcha know!" A cannon-like blast of laughter.

I waited for it to subside before commenting "But I want this part, Great-Uncle Leo. Anyhow, how did you hear about it? There hasn't been any publicity."

In response, a second blast of laughter bellowed out of the earpiece and into the secretary's office.

Followed by a loud crackling. "Oops! Cell phone's breaking up."

Then — a dial tone. Frowning, I replaced the receiver.

In the last years of his life, Dad had been an alcoholic. Drink had finally killed him: he'd crashed his car into a tree and died instantly.

However, when sober he was very entertaining and had told the best stories. Like, about all his relatives back east. I remembered these well.

Never, not once, did I remember him mentioning an Uncle Leo.

4.
The marvelous moonstone

"Probably a reporter," guessed Cindi Kahn. "That's the kind of thing reporters do. Pretend to be someone else so they can track down a story."

"But he was threatening me," I said. "I never heard of a reporter doing that."

Cindi shrugged and rolled her bulging eyes away from the stage, where we were sitting with the rest of the cast, to the dozen or so reporters in the audience seats. Jon and Mr. Murdock, the dumpling-shaped producer, were having an evening news conference to publicize the upcoming play.

"And may I present the true star of *The Moonstone*," oozed Mr. Murdock.

Mr. Murdock could only speak in rapid bursts, a breathing problem brought on by pollution he'd explained to us. Cindi and I thought it was brought on by his tubbiness, but of course we had to keep this opinion private: a producer is the one who funds a play.

Mr. Murdock waddled to center stage, into the spotlight that a stagehand had positioned there for him. Then, wheezing, Mr. Murdock pulled a velvet box from his pocket.

"By 'star' I refer not to the actors of this production, worthy though they are," and Mr. Murdock made a dipping motion of his round body towards us. His attempt at a bow, I supposed.

The producer flipped the box open. The obedient stagehand, wherever he or she was, zeroed the spotlight in on the ring inside.

Appreciative gasps from all directions. Cindi let out one of her screams.

The stone on the ring was a huge, pale, silvery white. Luminous as the moon that had hung over Granville Street the other night, I thought.

"Murdock Jewelers' finest moonstone," Mr. Murdock announced, after an annoyed glance back at Cindi for screaming. "Too priceless to sell. I keep it on display, under heavy guard, at my downtown store."

Recovering his good humor, he beamed at the photographers clustering by the stage's rim. Flash! Flash! They snapped the moonstone. After a while Mr. Murdock held up a pudgy forefinger to halt them, and oozed: "However, the famous Murdock moonstone will venture out into the world for my production of *The Moonstone*. The ring will appear on the gracious hand of Cindi Kahn, playing Miss Verinder!"

Applause and whistles. Cindi launched a scream of delight, but she clapped one of her gracious hands over her mouth and managed to smother it into a squeal.

Piano Man, who'd been tinkling out "Blue Moon," stepped forward to gape rather hungrily at the moonstone.

"What about security?" a reporter piped up. "You're not worried about theft? About an inside job, Mr. Murdock?"

Mr. Murdock replied coldly to the reporter, "There's no question of an 'inside job,' as you crudely put it. Impossible!"

Inside job. Suddenly I thought of Beak-Nose and her smug comment into her cell phone the other night. *Soon we'll be on the inside.*

I sat up straight, the way my singing instructor kept urging me to. In my mind I had just heard an echo of Beak-Nose. A hearty, jovial echo.

Great-Uncle Leo had asked, *So, yer not in yet, are ya?*

That was the remark of his that had bothered

me. I mean, aside from the truly scary one about my staying in the show being dangerous and bad for my health.

In. Inside. "Incredible," I murmured.

Both this Leo guy and Beak-Nose Bridey talked the same jargon.

Thief jargon.

Mr. Murdock beckoned Cindi forward. To yet more flashing bulbs, he slid the moonstone ring on one of her long, slender fingers. "Oooo!" Cindi cooed, bending her hand this way and that. The moonstone changed shades, creamy to cloudy to shadowy, as if it were changing moods.

Maybe there was a man in the moonstone as well as in the moon, I thought.

If so, he'd better watch his back. Away from its heavily guarded display case, the Murdock moonstone would be ripe for stealing.

"I think you're being imaginative," Jon said gently when I related my theory to him and Mother after the press conference. "Which is great, mind you, for someone in the creative arts."

Uh-oh. When a grown-up starts off with a compliment, you know a lecture is going to follow. Ms. Chen did this all the time. *Now, Dinah, it's a pleasure to see a child with so much energy. But ...*

"But," said Jon, "Violet Bridey — Angela's aunt — isn't a thief. The only thing she's ever stolen is scenes; she's an actress herself. Been in the theater for years. Mrs. Bridey specializes in villainess roles." Jon winked at me. "Maybe she never got over playing them. She has kind of a forbidding quality, doesn't she? I can't see Violet Bridey pulling off any heists, though."

He and Mother laughed. Very irritating of them. I myself could easily see Beak-Nose Bridey as a real-life thief. Tucking other people's valuables into her bird's nest of a bun, say. Then slipping away with scornful sniffs.

I tugged at Mother's coat sleeve. She was far too busy giggling at Jon's wit and growing pink-cheeked. "What about this Leo dude?" I pointed out. "You admitted you'd never heard of a Leo in Dad's family."

"Lots of Geminis, however," Mother joked.

Wait a minute. Mother — joking? Mothers weren't supposed to *joke*. I scowled and she hugged me. "I'm sorry, honey. I truly don't like the idea of some weirdo phoning you up and questioning you. In fact, I think I'll drive you to school and pick you up for a few weeks. You never know — he might be a stalker."

She looked worried. Now *that's* what mothers were supposed to do.

"Not a stalker," I corrected. "A thief. Leo, I mean," I said in a louder voice because Mother and Jon seemed to be ignoring me.

"This is the downside of celebrity," Mother was sighing to Jon. "The prank caller must've read the *Vancouver Sun* story on young performers a couple of weeks ago. Our Dinah was featured. 'The loudest of Vancouver's young performers,' the story described her.

"It also referred to the fact that Dinah's father died a couple of years ago. I suppose 'Leo' read that and decided to pose as a long-lost great-uncle. To get his kicks by scaring her," Mother added in disgust.

"A kick in the head, specifically," I said, but of course this went unheard. For the loudest of Vancouver's young performers, I sometimes had a lot of trouble getting listened to.

"I'll arrange for a cab to take Dinah to the theater every day," Jon was assuring Mother. "And I'll bring her home myself." He held Mother's hand for a moment. "I'll make sure the only thing that stalks Dinah is the celery we offer the cast and crew for snacks, along with carrots, pizza and potato chips."

Mother giggled again. I rolled my eyes at the man in the moon. After all, no one else was paying attention to me.

He hovered just off the ledge of Madge's balcony, over our rambling old house up the hill from Commercial Drive.

At night the Drive was always bustling, with jazz clubs, restaurants, and street musicians strumming and singing. Oh, and ambulance and police sirens, just to keep things lively. None of this bustle carried up the hill; our fluffy white-and-pumpkin-colored cat, Wilfred, was able to sleep in total tranquility on Madge's bedspread.

The only sound in Madge's room was the crackle of her burnished red hair. She was brushing it in front of the spindly, elegant vanity she'd found in a secondhand store on Main Street. My sister had a good eye for hunting down treasures. She was an artist and would probably go to art college in the fall.

Where, I mused, flipping through her prom fashion magazine, she'd become even more dreamy and abstract. Myself, I preferred hunting down criminals.

Like Beak-Nose. It was so obvious she was up to something sinister. Why did grown-ups always miss the point?

I examined a photo of a young woman in a prom dress of flesh-colored silk. Except that most of the flesh color she was exhibiting appeared to be skin. I cleaned my glasses with the edge of

Madge's quilt for a better look. Yup. There was a definite minimum of silk. Maybe this get-up was for girls who could only afford a bit of cloth.

I held up the magazine. "I hope you're not going to choose *this* outfit, Madge. I can lend you some money out of my piggy bank to buy a warmer one."

"Ninety-nine ... one hundred ... " Madge set down her silver brush — another of her antique shop finds — and smiled at me. "Don't worry, Dinah. I'm planning to design and sew something myself, in basic black."

"Huh? Why are you wasting your time on this stuff, then?" I fanned the pages: a rainbow of dresses flitted by. At the sound of riffling paper, Wilfred woke up, took fright and dashed from the room. (Wilfred was notoriously cowardly, even for a cat.)

"I look at them for ideas. For fun," said Madge. Climbing into bed, she prodded her feet at me from under the covers. I tumbled off the bed. "There," said Madge, stretching out comfortably. "You see, Dinah, my role model is Coco Chanel. Designing fashions at a time when clothes were frilly, Chanel invented the most elegant dress of all. It was almost severe in its simplicity. The little black dress. But she certainly would have studied the contemporary styles, just as I'm doing. To know what to reject, that is."

I got up off the floor and clutched my head. "Madge, please," I begged. "No more of this artistic stuff. I mean, you've just used up a half-minute of my life that I can never, never get back again."

Madge laughed. "Sorry, Di. I'll try to control myself." She picked up the prom fashion magazine.

I scrambled up onto the bed again, though safely out of range of her feet. Purring, Wilfred jumped on the quilt to snuggle between us. He knew a good opportunity for petting when he saw one.

"Now, Madge," I said sternly. I obliged Wilfred by scratching him around his fluffy head and under his ears with their wisps of fur sticking out. "I have something *real* to discuss with you. Mother. She's been behaving very oddly. Not Mother-like at all."

Madge tsked at a photo of a prom dress with a ballooning hem and huge silk flowers glued all over. "Hmm? Mother? Oh, she's probably showing the effects of studying so hard. This is her last year of courses, and she faces grueling finals in April." She turned away from the prom dress that had offended her taste to a page featuring advice on prom makeup.

"Yeah ... " I said doubtfully.

"Maybe Mother's acting giddy because she's stressed out," I acknowledged, as Wilfred stretched on his back for a tummy rub. "Oh, well, just a few more months now."

Madge glanced up. "Giddy?" she repeated. "Explain, please, small fry."

I groaned. *Small fry* was an expression she'd picked up from her boyfriend, Jack French, who was currently visiting family back east. A nice guy. Cool, even. But calling me *small fry* was a definite lapse in taste.

"Earth to Dinah," Madge persisted.

"Oh. Yeah, the giddy thing. Mother's been *giggling*." I paused for the effect of this shocking statement to sink in. "At Jon's lame jokes. Like, about the sinister Mrs. Bridey, whom I seriously suspect of being a thief. I'm positive Beak-Nose has her beady eyes fixed on the moonstone. The ring, I mean, not the play."

Madge held up a slim, delicate hand fragrant with eau de jasmine or whatever it was she was dousing herself with these days. "Time-out, please. And let's rewind. Are you referring to Jon as in Jon Horowitz, your director?"

"Well, not john as in the toilet." I hooted at this witticism. Alarmed, Wilfred abandoned his tummy rub to leap over Madge and stare at me reproachfully from behind her pillows.

"Mother was giggling with — Jon?" Madge sat up, her blue eyes clouding with concern. "This is bad, Dinah. Very bad. He must be ten years younger than she is. I can't believe this! Mother's going to make a complete fool of herself. I'd better talk to her."

Scrambling out of bed, she grabbed her housecoat off the back of the vanity chair and hurried down the hall to the little room we used as an office. Mother was in there, typing away at an essay about the history of book cataloguing. Or was it about the cataloguing of history books? I couldn't remember.

"What is it with teenaged girls?" I demanded of Wilfred. "I was trying to have a rational conversation with her about jewel thieves. Instead, she starts ranting about the age difference between Mother and Jon. Who cares? I mean, they're both *old*."

5.
On the trail of Beak-Nose

Madge was still at it the next morning at breakfast. "Are you sure there's nothing between you?" she asked Mother over scrambled eggs, toast and blueberry jam, all of which I, at least, was actually eating.

"Madge, stop worrying. I'm quite aware that Jon Horowitz is younger than I am. Besides, my goodness, if I fancied a man I'd get my hair done and buy some new clothes." Mother cast a rueful glance down at her gray, frayed sweats. "The only man in my life right now is Thomas Dewey."

Unstable. Given to wild accusations, I scribbled on a blank page of my math homework book under the heading "Madge: The Notes." Swigging back some milk, I kept a stern gaze on her over the rim of the glass. I planned to e-mail "Madge: The Notes" to Jack. Maybe he'd realize that she needed his stabilizing presence here in Vancouver.

I then spooned another layer of jam over my toast. Otherwise the bread taste interfered with the blueberries, I found. "So, who's this Dewey guy?" I demanded.

Mother explained, "He invented a way of cataloguing books. Using decimals."

"Oh. *Math*," I said witheringly. I flipped back a page in my math homework book and surveyed an utterly baffling question on meters and kilometers. Needless to say, I hadn't completed it last night. Instead I'd drawn a cartoon of myself tossing a towel on top of the question. As in, throwing in the towel. Maybe this would give nervous Mr. Paigely a laugh. Loosen him up a little.

"Now, Dinah," said Mother. "Madge will be walking you to school, and I'll be picking you up. Remember, we agreed," as I started to object through a mouthful of blueberry jam, "because of that odd phone call you received. The phony-great-uncle one."

"Now, Mother." I waved another jam-thick piece of toast around to imply that her idea itself should be waved off. "I'll walk home with Pantelli, as usual. I don't want you to interrupt your studies. I'll get him to walk me right to our door."

I could see Mother beginning to soften; after all, Lord Bithersby Elementary was just down the hill. Unfortunately, getting carried away as I often do, I plunged on. "Plus, Pantelli's been taking Tae Kwon Do. Any phony great-uncles come up to us — chop, chop, chop!" I made a series of vigorous gestures that resulted in half the piece of toast breaking off to fly *splat!* onto Madge's pearl-gray silk blouse.

She unstuck it slowly, glaring at me all the while. *Bad-tempered*, I wrote in "Madge: The Notes."

Without removing her baleful scowl from me, Madge informed Mother, "Dinah wants to sneak away after school and do some of her 'investigating.' She believes she's onto a gang of jewel thieves."

Venjful, I wrote. "Actually, I think it's a duo of jewel thieves," I said. I scrutinized *venjful*. Somehow it didn't look quite right. Maybe it was spelled *venchful*. I changed it. "See, Beak-Nose was phoning someone the night of the audition. Her accomplice, in my opinion."

Mother was horrified, as Madge had intended her to be. "Dinah, there is to be no investigating after school, or before it, for that matter. The notion of chop-chop-chopping at people! I've a good mind to phone Mrs. Audia and let her know the result of Pantelli's Tic Tac Toe lessons, or whatever they're called: that they give him violent urges."

"Pantelli only chops the air, Mother," I said.

"You know, *practice* chops. He hasn't chopped any people yet. Frankly, I doubt he'd chop Beak-Nose. She's your age, Mother — gosh, maybe even older. Chopping her wouldn't be very sporting."

Madge covered her ears and shrieked, "WILL YOU PLEASE STOP TALKING ABOUT 'CHOPPING'!" She ran upstairs.

Prone to emotional outbursts, I wrote.

"Oh dear, I'd better go calm her down," Mother fretted.

She hurried upstairs after Madge. With great satisfaction I reached for their toast. No one could clear a room like I could.

Pantelli was always ready to help with investigations. "Jewel thieves? Cool! Do they live around here? We can climb a tree and spy on 'em."

Our neighborhood was thick with horse chestnut trees, and Pantelli was an expert scaler of them. He loved trees. In the nice weather he spent as much time up there as he did in his own house. Nestled on a comfortable branch, he listened to CDs on his portable player, read comics and even snacked. If you happened to walk through a hailstorm of peanut shells, you could be pretty sure Pantelli was somewhere in the overhanging foliage. He'd proposed to his mother a plan for ropes and pulleys so she could bring out his meals for him to hoist up, but she'd drawn the line at that.

"Beak-Nose lives near Kitsilano beach," I whispered as, at the front of the classroom, Mr. Paigely called for order. "I looked up her address."

"Hmmm. Beach area." Pantelli rubbed his chin. "What kind of tree is common there?"

Mr. Paigely asked, "Does anyone know another national song for Canada besides our anthem, 'O Canada?'"

"Maples," mused Pantelli.

Mr. Paigely's thin, bespectacled face brightened. "Bravo, Pantelli! Before 'O Canada' was written, people often sang 'The Maple Leaf Forever.' Splendid," and he made a little check on the chart he used to track class participation.

When his shock at being praised had faded, Pantelli took on an irritating, smug expression. To put a stop to this, I found a sharp pencil in my case and jabbed his hand with it.

"I've been forbidden to go anywhere before or after school," I whispered.

"Bummer," Pantelli whispered back, massaging his skin.

"So we'll have to go *during*," I said.

An opportunity soon presented itself. "The museum!" announced Mr. Paigely, as our class charged out of the cars that various parent volunteers had brought us in. "The word 'museum' comes from 'muse,' or 'thinker' ... " His voice trailed off. Ignoring him, we were all racing each other to the Vancouver Museum's glass entry doors. Mr. Paigely ran after us, flapping the handouts we were supposed to use in touring the exhibits.

"People!" he pleaded. Anxious to avoid receiving the handouts, everyone was speeding away. Once you got a handout, you'd be obligated to fill in answers.

Pantelli and I hung back behind a kiosk until Mr. Paigely and the kids he was chasing receded deep into the museum. "Okay," I said. "Let's sleuth."

Beak-Nose lived a few blocks from the museum. "Yeah, lots of maples around here," Pantelli said appreciatively as we started off. "Did you know there are 150 types of maple? Just a few in Canada, among them the sugar, black, silver, big leaf, red, mountain, striped, Douglas, vine and Manitoba."

"Interesting," I said politely, though I hoped Pantelli wouldn't proceed on to the rest of the 150 worldwide. You never knew with him.

We reached an ivy-covered house inky with the shade of maple trees. As we hesitated on the sidewalk, a crisp golden maple leaf fluttered down from a branch. Pantelli caught it and, entranced, studied its veins.

"So, what's your plan?" he asked.

"Oh, I don't actually make *plans*," I said. Then, to show him that plan-lessness wasn't a problem for me, I marched up the walk and onto the dark porch. Not that I'd figured out a course of action or anything like that, but at least I *looked* purposeful.

Beside the door, four intercom buttons were set into a metal panel. A label with "V. BRIDEY" printed in black ink was stuck next to the button marked 201.

So far I'd failed to learn anything the phone book hadn't already told me.

I glanced round, desperate enough for ideas to ask Pantelli's advice.

He was nowhere to be seen. The branches of the maple tree closest to the house rustled wildly. I called up, "Some help you are!"

"Well, sorrrreeee!" a voice — not Pantelli's — snapped in return. A cross-looking postman strode up the porch steps. He bore a heavy mailbag that bent his lean frame to one side. I had to tip my head to the same side to view him straight.

"Always the same," the postman fumed, jangling a massive set of keys at me. "Lock yourself out due to sheer carelessness, and expect the letter carrier to let you back in. Sure, you're fast enough to complain about postal service, but when there's the slightest trouble it's the postman you expect to bail you out!"

Unlocking the door, he whipped it open angrily. "Th-thanks," I said and stepped in ahead of him.

The hall was dingy, with a single, pale pod light overhead. In case the postman was watching, I headed with phony confidence up the worn mahogany staircase to the second level and V. BRIDEY in 201.

I needn't have worried about the postman. Still busy complaining, he flung open the first mail-slot door and rammed envelopes in, crumpling them badly.

Upstairs, another pale pod light shone feebly. Beneath it, the mahogany floor had a wan gleam — and ferocious creaks. I gave up trying to be stealthy and hurried right over to the door marked 201.

I jammed an ear against the door.

On the other side of the door — SQUA-A-W-WK!

Ow, my eardrum.

Then: "You're so amusing, darling. That's what I adore about you."

Beak-Nose, all right. That squawk had been a laugh. My ear was still ringing.

A male voice mumbled something. It sounded as if he was complaining.

"Now, don't be a sulk, sweetie," cajoled Beak-Nose. She was easy to hear. Her voice had the jangling clarity of an alarm clock going off. "I almost got my reluctant little niece into *The Moonstone*. If it hadn't been for that chubby loud-mouth, I'd have been backstage on opening night to carry out our clever scheme."

The man said something. I caught a few words: " ... gotta be a way ... "

"Darling. Lovey Pie. I'll find another way, won't I?"

More mumbling by Beak-Nose's male friend.

Then Beak-Nose, suddenly sharp and not Lovey-Pie-ish at all. "Well, your silly phone call didn't work, did it?" she demanded scornfully. "'Uncle' Leo, my foot," she added.

His silly phone call ... the guy with her must be Leo!

Her foot, my neck. After leaning against the door so long, my neck was acquiring a definite crick. I stood up and moved my head up and down, side to side.

Unfortunately, I brushed against the brass door-knob of 201. It rattled.

Uh-oh. I ran to the landing, but not before

Beak-Nose swept her door open in a grandly dramatic gesture. "Who — ? Why, it's you," she snapped. The tip of her beak nose quivered with suspicion. "What are you doing here?"

"Um," I said. "Girl Guide cookie-selling?"

Beak-Nose was unamused, since I had neither boxes of cookies nor order forms. She wrapped her long, crimson silk dressing gown closer about her and moved towards me. The silk made rustles, like hissing.

It occurred to me that the hall was awfully quiet. All the other apartment dwellers must be at work.

Then I realized that, out of nervousness, I was still rolling my head around. I gave Beak-Nose a fake, teeth-bared smile and said, "With this disability I have, it's hard to focus on address numbers. I was actually looking for the museum. See ya."

And I bolted.

In case she and Leo were watching from the window, I continued to roll my head around outside.

"Cool," commented Pantelli's voice from the golden and red depths of the maple leaves. "You musta seen *The Exorcist* too. The best part is when, after spinning her head like you're doing, the girl barfs green bile."

Pantelli shinnied to the lowest branch. Swinging ape-like from it, he inquired with interest, "Is that what you're planning to do next?"

I glanced back at the house — and, as I did, a crimson-sleeved hand wrenched curtains across the window of 201.

I stopped rotating my head. "I was eavesdropping," I informed Pantelli. "After I cunningly infiltrated the place, that is."

"Eavesdropping on who?" Pantelli demanded. "That dude in the chair?"

I stopped short, even though we needed to make tracks back to the museum. "You saw the dude?"

"Yeah, o' course. Through the window. Your friend, too — boy, that beak nose really stands out."

"That 'dude' was Leo! What did he look like?"

"Uh ... "

"C'mon," I said impatiently. "Young, old, what?"

Pantelli frowned. "Uh, y'know. In the middle."

"Tall, short? Fat, thin? Bald?"

"Oh, not bald," Pantelli assured me. "Medium-colored hair, I'd say. And the rest — medium everything." He beamed at me, pleased with his report.

Too bad Beak-Nose had shut the curtains, or I would've shinnied up the maple myself. Pantelli was hopeless!

6.
Clackety-clack, better turn back

The next day was the first rehearsal of *The Moonstone*. I was at center stage, singing "Blue Moon." As Coretta Cuff, I was missing my dad, who was far away in India. On one side of me was Cindi, as Miss Verinder, wondering if her fiancé really loved her.

On my other side was Frank Murdock, the actor playing Miss Verinder's fiancé.

Yup, Frank Murdock, as in a relative of Mr. Murdock's. The producer's nephew, in fact. Surprise, surprise that Frank got the part when he auditioned.

I was prepared to dislike Frank intensely because of this family connection. I mean, go out and audition for a part based on your abilities, like the rest of us!

Anyhow, when Cindi stopped singing her part

of "Blue Moon," Frank would take over. As Miss Verinder's fiancé, he was wondering if *she* really loved *him*.

In my opinion, the engaged couple must be pretty stupid, but Jon had assured me this type of misunderstanding happens all the time in plays.

For the last part of "Blue Moon," our three voices, Cindi's, Frank's and mine, were to come together from the different places onstage. It'd be a rousing finale to the scene.

At the moment, we were nowhere near rousing. "Dinah," Jon interrupted me, "I need more emotion. Your mind isn't on Coretta. You're blasting the notes out with total indifference, like a trumpet being played by an oxygen tank. Music is more than notes, kid. It's feeling. Emotion."

It was true that my mind wasn't on Coretta. It was on Beak-Nose Bridey and the mysterious Leo. On the fact that they were so eager to get "inside" the production of *The Moonstone*.

But who *was* Leo?

With difficulty I brought myself back to the role of Coretta.

"I'm ready," I said to Jon. He nodded, Piano Man started up again and I filled my voice with the genuine anxiety I was feeling about Beak-Nose, Leo and the ring I was sure they wanted to steal.

"Great, great," Jon encouraged. At last satisfied with my performance, he switched his concentration to Cindi. On high notes she was forgetting to sing. Instead, she screamed. I guess it was just too much a habit with her.

I noticed Piano Man check his watch. Between screams/high notes, he called to Jon, "Hey, it's lunch. Mind if we break?"

"Sure," said Jon. "Cindi, will you stay a minute? I need to talk to you about the character of Rachel."

Poor Cindi. Piano Man had his priorities straight. FOOD. He and the other cast and crew headed off to lunch at one of the nearby cafés.

I, on the other hand, had a lunchbox waiting in the cloakroom. Thanks to Leo, Mother had forbidden me to leave the theater unless Jon accompanied me.

Which, to be fair, he often did, topping up the already generous lunches Mother packed with California rolls or frozen yogurt or double chocolate brownies that he bought for me in addition to buying his own lunch.

Today, though, it looked like he'd be too busy toning down Cindi.

I was about to thunder down the stage steps — I mean, thundering is what you do with steps, right? — when Frank Murdock whispered, "Hey!"

He strolled up to me, smiling. He had a nice, sleepy kind of smile, and green eyes that twinkled. "Great set of pipes you've got there, kid. Like Streisand, only more down-to-earth. A really honest sound."

He'd lost me. Heck, I just opened my mouth and sang. But suddenly I knew he meant all this. Genuinely. And that meant a lot to *me*. "Thanks," I said, smiling back at him.

Maybe he wasn't so bad, even if he *was* a Murdock.

I huddled comfortably in one of the lobby chairs. I was about to bite into my favorite type of sandwich — banana, peanut butter and honey — when Jon's assistant called, "Message for you, Dinah."

"Huh?" I withdrew the sandwich from my open mouth and looked at her over my comic book, *Ultra-Homicidal Deathstalkers*.

The assistant, who was always very harried, dropped a phone-message paper on top of a picture of an octopus wielding a sword in each tentacle.

"Ew," shuddered Jon's assistant at the sight of the octopus. She rushed off.

I bit into my banana, peanut butter and honey sandwich and read the note: *Madge says she'll buy you lunch at the Windmill Café, close by.*

Madge was in the area. Cool. I stuffed *Ultra-Homicidal Deathstalkers* into my jeans pocket and went outside. Madge was probably submitting her portfolio to Emily Carr Art College, just down on Granville Island. She was applying to go there next year.

The Windmill Café wasn't as close by as all that. I found out from asking a hot dog vendor that it was across Granville Street, up a half block and along a garbage-strewn lane. The kind of place, in other words, that your mother would not want you to be alone in.

I hesitated. I knew Madge would be waiting in the café, but occasionally mothers had a point. The lane felt too lonely for comfort. Chased by the breeze, a torn, muddied plastic grocery bag skipped along the broken pavement towards me. Beside a Dumpster, an abandoned grocery cart, buffeted by the same breeze, rattled fiercely.

Suddenly, from behind the Dumpster, a grimy hand shot out. I opened my mouth to scream — being around Cindi was starting to have an effect on me — when I realized the hand had appeared only to still the grocery cart.

The hand retreated again. Whoever, or, I thought nervously, *what*ever owned it most likely wasn't interested in me.

I spotted the faded sign for the Windmill Café. I walked towards it, glancing around me all the while. The streets at both ends of the lane were much too distant. I could see cars going by, but the backs of the buildings muffled traffic sounds.

"Tsk, tsk!"

I jumped, thinking someone was clacking his or her tongue in disapproval at me.

"Tsk, tsk!"

Not a someone. A something. A miniature windmill, nailed over the café door. Its blades were making the noise: they spun in the breeze, *clackety-clack, better turn back*.

Okay, so that last bit was my imagination. Get a grip, Dinah. You're about to see your sister. Besides, this is a busy city in broad daylight.

Taking a deep breath, I twisted the black doorknob and stepped into an interior that wasn't either broad or lighted.

I peered round the cramped, dark café. Its few rickety round tables had nobody sitting at them.

From a teeny hallway shuffled a pale, sad-faced young man in black turtleneck and pants. He dragged himself over to a teeny counter. Even in the dim light I could see a solid coating of dust on the countertop.

The young man didn't acknowledge me, though by now I was staring pointedly at him from the other side of the counter. I said loudly, "I'M WITH NASA. WE'RE TRYING TO DETECT SIGNS OF LIFE IN THIS PLACE. HAVE YOU SEEN ANY?"

The young man sighed and massaged his temples, as if a bad headache were coming on. "Everybody's a comedian. Like, I don't know why you're not in school. If you're going to play hooky, why, like *why*, did you have to choose the Windmill Café? Nobody else does, as you can see. But," he threw up his pale hands in resignation, "whatever."

"I'm looking for a tall, auburn-haired girl," I said.

"Aren't we all, though."

He sat on a stool and rested his head, left cheek down, on the counter. The earrings in his left ear let out a long series of tinkles as they met the hard surface.

He hadn't laughed at my joke, so I saw no reason to laugh at his. "Mind if I check the place out?" I asked.

"Yeah, whatever." He closed his eyes.

I headed into the teeny hallway. There was a door, ajar, on which a scribbled sign had been thumbtacked: WASHROOM – WOMEN, MEN & WHATEVER. At the end of the hallway, a door to the outside had a square window that you'd probably once been able to see through.

That door, too, was ajar. Which made me think of the old riddle, *When is a door not a door?*

It made me think of something else. Madge might have stepped out for a breath of fresh air. But it was also possible that another person had stepped in, unnoticed.

But where would they be, in these teeny surroundings? The options were pretty limited.

I realized the answer to that question too late.

Fast, thudding footsteps came from behind, out of the WOMEN, MEN & WHATEVER door. A heavy, coarse blanket swooped over me, blinding me and muffling my breath.

Not that I just took this. I punched, clawed, kicked and yelled.

"YEOW," yelped — Leo! I'd have known that hearty, jovial voice anywhere. "Yer a tough lil' cookie. Ain't that a kick in the head! Why ain't you getting the message, toots. Drop outta the show *fer yer own good*. Now, you gotta learn ta mind yer own beeswax, kiddo. No more snoopin' around Mrs. Bridey. You kin spend some time locked up in here. Some nice quiet time," he jeered, "thinking 'bout what I just said. Let this be a warnin' to ya, hokay?"

He shoved me into the teeny washroom.

I'd pulled part of the blanket off by now. I struck out wildly and clamped onto an orange-and-green plaid pocket.

"Why, you lil' — " A sweaty hand closed about my wrist. The harder he wrenched at it, trying to free himself from the clutch of my hand, the harder I clung to his pocket.

Then he started pressing the door against my arm at the same time as he was yanking at my wrist. "YEOW," I yelped, not sure that an amputated arm was worth the struggle of holding on to the old plaid. But, in one last effort, I grasped the pocket's inside even more tightly.

R-r-r-i-i-p! The pocket came off. I lost my balance and fell backward into the washroom. I had a brief glimpse of bushy gray hair and orange-and-green plaid over a paunchy stomach — and the door slammed on me.

"Har har," Leo chuckled from the other side. I heard the squeaks of something being dragged, followed by a scrabbling noise against the door, then heavy footsteps thudding away.

"Just a domestic dispute," Leo called, presumably to the sad-faced young man. "Let her stew for a while. It's the latest in child therapy."

I tried the door. It wouldn't budge against

whatever he'd propped up on the other side.

I was trapped.

Okay, not long-term trapped, but long enough. By the time the young man from the counter pried the chair away from the door and let me out, I was gulping back deep gasps and heaving out long, noisy breaths.

"Whoa," he exclaimed. "Do you have asthma or whatever?"

I pushed past him scornfully. "I was getting ready to start singing," I informed him. "Last time I got locked into a small, enclosed space, I belted out "After You've Gone" till somebody heard me."

"You mean this happens to you a lot?" He started to scratch his head; then a fingernail snagged in one of his earrings. Grimacing, he struggled to ease it out.

At this point I really couldn't be bothered to launch into an autobiography. Instead I demanded, "Can you describe that guy to me?"

"You mean he's not related to you? Huh." The young man freed his fingernail and examined it sadly. It was now broken. "Um ... well ... fat."

"Tall? Short? Or ... ?"

The young man shrugged. "Or whatever."

7.
On the sushi menu:
a co-detective

When I arrived, panting, in the lobby, I asked the receptionist exactly who had phoned. "A woman. Said she was your sister," the receptionist had answered in surprise. "Didn't you get the message?"

Oh, I'd got the message all right. It had been Beak-Nose who'd phoned, pretending to be Madge. She'd set me up into getting a good scare from Leo.

Everyone was waiting for me. Lectures were brewing in Jon's mild gray eyes. Mr. Wellman, my agent, had warned me never, but *never*, to be late for rehearsal.

"I'm sorry," I said weakly. "I got stuck in a washroom."

"You left the building," said Jon. "When I call a break, it's a short break. As well as disrespecting the rest of the cast, you flouted your mother's concerns about your safety. C'mon, Dinah. You know the rules. You don't go off on your own."

Going off on my own had been the least part of it, I thought. But if I explained, Mother would for sure pull me from the play.

Jon turned to Piano Man, who was, as usual, chomping on a toothpick. "'Blue Moon,' from the top."

Cindi blinked her goggly eyes at me in sympathy. "You weren't very late," she reassured me.

Frank winked. "Not to worry. Coupla years from now you'll be a big star and you can get temperamental and walk off any set you choose."

I giggled. "I don't want to be temperamental. I'm not even sure I want to be a 'big star.' I just want to sing."

"Good," commented Jon, overhearing this last part. Piano Man was cuing me. "You're on," said Jon.

At the end of the day, Mother came to pick me up. She complimented Cindi on her screaming, which she'd heard from the parking lot. They started gabbing in the red velvet lobby, while I stood on one foot, then another, to prevent prickles charging up and down my legs. It's so dull when grown-ups get going.

Frank sauntered up and began to make me giggle by whispering things about Cindi. What wide eyes she had, and how they were melting his heart. What a sweet voice she had, like a running brook — except when she was screaming, of course. "Though *you* could probably out-sing one of her screams," he predicted. "Nobody would even think of her."

By now Cindi, aware as people always are when others are talking about them, was blushing. "Okay, guys. What gives?"

"Scream," I told her.

And, well-trained by our agent, Mr. Wellman, she did. Automatically. The scream's single, piercing note whipped through the lobby, shaking the red velvet folds of the curtains and rattling the photos of the famous actors and actresses who'd performed there.

"Huh," I told Frank, who was regarding Cindi in awe. "That ain't nothin'."

And I launched into a middle C that reduced Cindi's scream to a tinny whine. Above us, disturbed by the double blast of our voices, chandelier prisms jangled.

Since she'd let loose before I did, Cindi's scream faded ahead of my middle C. I just kept going. I was having fun.

Jon popped into the lobby. He drew his finger across his throat — I stopped. "What's going on?" he demanded.

Then he saw Mother. "Oh, hi," he said. The anger disappeared from his face and suddenly he looked very young. "Excuse me if I sounded out of sorts, Suzanne. Things get a little frenetic around here."

I stared at Jon, wondering if Cindi's and my blasts had blown a few of his brain fuses. *Things?* That, I presumed, meant me.

"I think we should all go for sushi," Jon suggested to Mother.

Oh, pardon me. To *Suzanne*.

"'We walked along Broadway,'" Frank sang, as we did just that, heading towards Jon's favorite sushi place. Except that this was Vancouver's Broadway, not the New York City Broadway Frank was singing about.

"Someday you'll sing on the big Broadway," Frank assured me. "You've got the voice, kid."

I was extremely flattered, but of course it wasn't cool to show pleasure at a compliment, so I just shrugged. I took the edge of my scarf and wiped the latest smudges off my glasses. "I couldn't go for a while," I said. "I have a case to solve."

"What, pray tell?" demanded Frank, so then I had to explain about Beak-Nose's suspicious phone call at the auditions, and Leo stuffing me into the Windmill Café washroom, and their plan, I believed, to steal the moonstone.

Mother and Jon were walking on ahead and didn't hear. The silvery puffs of air I'd breathed out with all my explaining separated them from the three of us, as if they were in a different dimension. Or did they seem that way because they were so intent on talking to each other?

Meanwhile Frank was making Cindi and me laugh hysterically. He knew Violet Bridey from performing with her, he said — and squished his features together so that his face became long and disapproving. "I am scornful about everything!" he informed passersby.

We giggled right to the door of Sushi Boat, not a real boat at all, but a second-story restaurant with some lame sails flapping wetly from the windows. "It's good, it's good," Jon called back, grinning at my expression. "In food if not in décor."

Mother smiled back at me, checking, as she did every few minutes or so, that I was all right. A motherly thing.

Weird how a mother's glances, even good-natured ones, have a way of sobering you up. Cindi and I both stopped giggling. Cindi whispered, "You better tell her what happened in the café."

Frank's green eyes, which had been merry, now clouded with indignation. "You're right, Cin. Let's tell Jon, too. This is no laughing matter. If Dinah's in danger, it's Jon's responsibility to look out for her. Why'd he let you go off on your own today, hon? I mean, he usually goes with you, right?" Frank gave me a hug. "I think we need to tell Jon what happened — and point out that it happened while you were in *his* care."

Cindi was gazing, besotted, at Frank. He sure was handsome when he got mad. I, however, was more preoccupied with what he'd just said. It was nice of Frank not to blame me for sneaking out of the theater, but come on, I told myself. It had been my choice to go AWOL. There was no way Jon could have suspected I was leaving the premises.

Besides, there was the little matter of me getting into trouble if I told Jon what had happened. Mega trouble, guaranteed, if he and Mother found out that I'd been tracking criminals down.

"Um, Frank," I said. "I don't want to say anything about this, to Mother or Jon. *Please*."

"Not even pretty please," said Frank, still looking stern. "Suzanne," he called up the stairs after Mother.

"No," I begged. "I promise I won't investigate Leo on my own anymore."

Frank hesitated. Mother had turned back to look down at us. He murmured, "We-ell, okay. No more Leo-chasing." He smiled. "Or Pisces-chasing or Aquarius-chasing, for that matter."

I rolled my eyes. *Everyone* was onto this joke. "I promise I won't tackle anyone single-handed," I murmured back.

"It's all right, Suzanne," Frank called to Mother. "We just had a minor crisis — uh, Cindi realized they don't cook their fish here."

"Oh," said Mother, giving Cindi a rather puzzled glance — we'd all known from the start we were going for sushi.

"That's settled, then, Ms. Galloway," Frank told me quietly. "Next time you feel an overwhelming urge to pursue Leo, take me along. I'll gettum," and Frank began throwing punches at an invisible adversary, complete with sound effects. "Try THAT on, buddy ... POW. BAM!"

"I hate to interrupt," Jon said acidly from the top of the stairs. "You may or may not be interested to know that our booth is ready."

Frank took one of my hands, Cindi the other and they swung me on the steps. We ran up. It wouldn't be at all bad to have a co-detective, I thought happily.

I mean, there was Pantelli, but at any given opportunity he'd forget about detecting to shinny up a tree.

"I have to admit I missed Pantelli at dinner," I told Madge later, as she did her hundred brushstrokes in front of the vanity mirror. Sprawled on her bed, I flipped idly through the now dog-eared prom fashion magazine. "The problem in eating with grown-ups at a sushi joint is that nobody wants to fence with you."

Madge paused in mid-stroke, eying me quizzically.

"Using chopsticks," I explained. It was all I could do not to sound impatient. How slow-witted could Madge get? "Nothing's more satisfying than a sword fight. Whoever cracks the other person's chopstick first, wins."

"How do you eat then?"

"With fingers. C'mon, Madge." I noticed that she shuddered. Maybe a cold breeze was filtering through her balcony door. "Anyhow, the sushi was good. 'Specially the tempura. I concentrated on that — my own and other people's, of course. Num."

"But all that breading, Dinah. Fattening!"

"Exactly," I agreed, smacking my lips at the memory of it.

In the magazine I found a survey titled "How

well do you communicate with your boyfriend?" Madge scorned surveys, but there was no reason I couldn't fill it out on her behalf. Hey! I'd mail it to Jack. My e-mailed "Madge: The Notes" message had earned a rude reply from him. But the answers I planned to give on this survey oughtta get him back here in a hurry.

"Brilliant. You are so brilliant," I mumbled to myself. I felt in my jeans pocket for a pencil and instead found my fingers closing round a scrap of cloth.

"So, what did everyone else have?" Madge inquired. She'd put down the brush and was reaching for one of a dozen jars of cream.

"Huh?" I withdrew the orange-and-green plaid cloth from my pocket. It was the pocket I'd clawed off Leo's jacket. I'd taken it out a few times to stare at it, convinced I'd seen it somewhere before.

"Oh, we had boats," I replied absently. "You know, wooden plates shaped like boats. Huge ones, stuffed with all kinds of sushi and sashimi. Frank and Cindi shared one. Mother and Jon did, too. I, naturally, had my own."

I stared at the cloth. It was faded and dirty. No wonder Leo was resorting to thievery, if the rest of his wardrobe looked like this. He badly needed to go shopping for new duds.

"Huh," I said thoughtfully. Madge wasn't the only one who was sometimes slow-witted. I was just now realizing where I'd seen this plaid before.

The night of the auditions. There'd been an old orange-and-green plaid jacket on the piano bench ... beside Piano Man.

Who was pudgy, like Leo.

"Will you stop saying *huh*!" Madge snapped.

I looked at her in surprise. Anyone would have: she sported a pink cream circle around each eye. I sniffed. Strawberry. "Not bad," I commented. "But I don't really see the point of using that as eye goo. Spread it on toast, maybe — "

I halted. Madge's gaze was blue fire. She demanded, "What do you mean, Mother and Jon shared a boat?"

I sighed. "Am I not getting through to you, Madge? A plate thing-y. It's just a gimmick that the restaurant uses because it's called Sushi Boat.

"The plate wasn't much of a boat," I added with scorn. "I tested it for waterproofness by pouring a bottle of soya sauce inside. It failed. So then I had this pool of sauce covering my placemat. Actually, the pool was kind of a neat shape. As an artist, you would have appreciated it."

Madge appeared ready to explode out of her circles of pink cream. "Dinah, are you *thick*? Don't you understand — when a male and female share a plate, even a boat-shaped plate, it means they're interested in each other! Romantically. Like the first time Jack and I went out on a date. We shared an appetizer of crab-stuffed mushroom caps."

"Uh, Madge, like I'm always trying to tell you, these are moments of my life that I'll never recapture ... "

Madge flounced off downstairs to warn Mother yet again about dating a younger man.

She needs Jack back, I thought. He'd know how to deal with her. They were both in that same weird age group. The tormented teens.

The "How well do you communicate with your boyfriend?" survey had to work. It just had to.

8.
Sour notes with Piano Man

First question.

Do you believe that your boyfriend understands you?

I chewed on the end of my pen. This always helped my creative juices flow for some reason, though Mother warned it might end up with ink flowing onto my tongue.

Okay. I had it. I put pen nib to paper.

"We must thank Dinah for being so creative," declared Mr. Paigely.

I glanced up, surprised and uneasy. It was next morning, in class, and I was taking a bit of time out of paying attention to fill in the boyfriend survey for Madge.

I hoped Mr. Paigely hadn't realized I was being inattentive. Maybe he was being sarcastic.

He was smiling at me. I smiled back, my phony,

bared-teeth smile. He wasn't being sarcastic, I realized. Mr. Paigely was too nice to be sarcastic.

"We must thank you for bringing to our attention the art of the mystery," he continued. "What is a 'mystery', uh, let's see ... Lee Ann?"

Phew. He was off me now, whatever he'd been blathering about. In answer to the first survey question I scribbled, *Does Jack understand me? No way, José! The guy goes back east! Like, what'm I, chopped liver?*

I chuckled to myself at the thought of Jack receiving the completed survey in the mail. However, my chuckles died a fast death as I noticed Mr. Paigely regarding me again. Along with everyone else in the class.

Uh-oh. He had that look of anticipation. He'd asked me something.

I put on my most scholarly expression: a frown, and a shoved-out lower lip. "I agree with you, Mr. Paigely," I said solemnly. Whatever the question had been, I hoped agreement was appropriate.

"Just so," the substitute teacher beamed. "Now tell us all about it."

"Oh, *it*," I said, with a falsely enthusiastic laugh. What on earth was he talking about? I shrugged. "Well ... y'know ... 'It'! I'd say ... Yup, I'd say 'it' pretty well speaks for itself." I beamed back at Mr. Paigely.

Laughs disguised as coughs erupted here and there around the classroom. Pantelli, who was reading up on rowan trees behind his language arts textbook, grinned at me.

Mr. Paigely hesitated in confusion. I felt a slight twinge of guilt: he was too nice to be suspicious of me.

"What do *you* think, Mr. Paigely?" I asked.

His thin face brightened. "The poet T.S. Eliot called *The Moonstone* 'the first and greatest of English detective novels.' Before its publication in 1868, novels had pretty much described the adventures of their characters as they happened. There'd be surprises, but no mystery hanging over the plot like a shadow. No blood-curdling suspense. No detective or red-herring suspects or shocking final plot twists."

Now I remembered. I'd been assigned to research *The Moonstone*. That had been "it." I chewed my pen some more, regretting that I hadn't at least started some research. What Mr. Paigely was saying was interesting. He'd become animated in talking about mysteries.

"We have Wilkie Collins to thank for introducing these classic mystery features," Mr. Paigely said. "Funnily enough, the *Moonstone* author's family pressured him to become a lawyer. They had no patience at all with his sinister scribblings. But Wilkie kept on, regardless. You see?" Mr. Paigely beamed round at us. "Have faith in what you love doing, and you'll succeed at it."

Cool stuff, even if Mr. Paigely did revert to being a regular teacher after that and instruct us to write a speech about our favorite activity. Teachers are wily that way.

Still, I had to admit I now kind of liked the guy. It had been neat to learn about Wilkie Collins and how he'd stayed true to his creative side. In a way, that had been what my Dad told me to do. *Your voice is your gift, Dinah,* he'd said. *Open up your voice as you would a package all wrapped in ribbons and bows — and use it. Celebrate it ...*

Meanwhile, I had another type of creativity to attend to. I resumed filling out the boyfriend survey, which I intended, with Madge's name on the return address, to mail to Jack that afternoon.

Question 3: Is there anything you're not telling your boyfriend?

I munched the end of my pen. *Yup,* I wrote. *With Jack out of town, I'm getting a mega crush on ...*

I hesitated. What good-looking guy could I mention?

Ah. Brilliant, Dinah.

... this cute guy named Frank Murdock. My

kid sister's in a play with him. Frank is one hot
tamale, I'll tell ya.

Wilkie Collins, I felt, would have been proud.

Meanwhile, there was Piano Man to follow up on.
Orange-and-green-plaid-wearing Piano Man, to be
specific. I remembered how hungrily he'd eyed the
moonstone ring at Mr. Murdock's press conference.

"Just how much do you know about Piano
Man?" I muttered to Jon.

I'd settled myself beside Jon in the audience
seats. Onstage, Piano Man warmed up for a song
Cindi was about to rehearse.

"Who, Graham?" said Jon, surprised. "I dunno
... he's been around the local theater scene for years.
When he's not involved with a play, he usually tinkles out tunes in piano bars."

"Or evilly plots jewelry heists," I responded in
ominous tones.

These were lost on Jon, busy making director-
type notes in the margin of his script.

Cindi hadn't appeared yet, so I sauntered down
the aisle to the stage's edge. The direct approach is
best, in my view. "I'm onto you," I informed Graham
the Piano Man.

Graham crashed out a discordant note and stared
at me, startled. "You — you are?" he stammered.

I scowled at him. "You betcha. I know what you did yesterday at lunch."

Graham stopped playing altogether and turned pale. "You do?"

I'd been right. He was Leo. "Well, of course," I retorted. "You oughtta be ashamed of yourself."

Graham looked unhappily down at the piano keys. "I am. I truly am. Just ... please ... just don't tell my wife."

"Huh?" I remembered Beak-Nose's cooed *Darling* and the crimson silk dressing gown she'd worn. For someone Graham's age, that get-up would probably be considered sexy. Yech.

"Your behavior is so-o-o shocking," I scolded Graham. "I wouldn't blame your wife if she divorced you."

My voice, as it tends to do, had grown rather loud. Everyone was staring at us.

Cindi walked onstage. "Why would Mrs. Morrison divorce him?" she demanded cheerfully. "Graham's a complete teddy bear."

"No way!" I protested. "Do you know what he did yesterday at lunch? He — "

Cindi giggled. "I know all about it."

My jaw embarked on a swift, stunned descent.

"Sure. He went off his diet." Cindi shrugged good-naturedly. "I was with him. After Jon finished coaching me, Graham, Frank and I popped into Dairy Queen and ordered the nummiest, most fattening items on their menu."

"If Griselda finds out, she'll be furious," Piano Man mourned. "She has me on this careful diet, which I promised I wouldn't go off."

Uh-oh. *Diet* was what Graham was feeling guilty about? No wonder he'd looked at the moonstone hungrily. It had probably reminded him of a nice, fat marshmallow.

And if Cindi and Frank had spent lunchtime with him yesterday at Dairy Queen, Graham had an alibi. He couldn't have ambushed me at the Windmill Café. He couldn't be Leo.

I bared my teeth in my best phony smile. With any luck, the cast and crew now staring at me would assume this had all been a friendly little joke.

Then I thought of something. I pulled a piece of the orange-and-green plaid from my pocket. "Isn't this from your jacket?" I accused.

Piano Man had been slouched sadly over his keyboard. At the sight of the plaid he shot up so fast he knocked the piano bench on its side. The bench lid opened and sheets of music poured out.

Graham's face was beet red. "How dare you," he spluttered. "How dare you suggest that I'd wear the Macdonald tartan when I'm a MORRISON!"

I maintained my phony, bared-teeth smile. "Well!" I exclaimed, trying to sound cheerful. "Looks like I made a MacStake!"

9.
Lady Macbeth and the strange blob

"No more investigating, Dinah," Mother said firmly. "What with school and the play, you have enough to concentrate on without inventing mysteries."

"But, Mother — "

"Dinah, we've had this conversation about twenty-eight times. Maybe you can waste your life on it, but I can't. I'm already middle-aged. I can't afford to use up any more of my own life hearing about this Bride of Dracula woman or whatever she is."

"Bridey," I clarified, viewing Mother with interest. She didn't usually get upset about things. Must be her upcoming exams — or hey. Maybe Madge was right. Maybe Mother was falling for Jon. Love had weird effects on people, I'd heard.

Memo to self: Never, but never, fall for anyone.

Meanwhile, my investigative work — which I

naturally had no intention of giving up — had stalled. I had no idea who Leo was. Sure, Leo's orange-and-green plaid jacket had been dumped on the piano bench on audition night. But it could have belonged to anyone. Theater people were notoriously messy, I was discovering. They dumped their stuff all over the place.

No wonder I felt so at home with them.

Luckily, an opportunity to unstall my investigations presented itself. The Vancouver theater community was having a festival day, downtown at the Roundhouse Center. My class, among many others, was going.

As Mrs. Audia, our parent volunteer, drove Pantelli, me and a couple of other kids downtown, I scanned the festival brochure Mr. Paigely had handed out.

One of the listings was: Violet Bridey: Readings from the part of Lady Macbeth.

"Whoa," I shouted. "Beak-Nose!"

Mrs. Audia, who, though pretty enough, had kind of a large schnozz, glanced round at me with an insulted expression.

I squinted to detect the real Violet Bridey beneath her thick white face paint and heavily darkened eyebrows and eyelids.

Beside me in the Roundhouse, Pantelli was also watching the actress, but with admiration, not suspicion.

"Boy, does she ever look creepy!"

"Ssssh!" someone hissed at him.

At that moment, Beak-Nose, seeming taller and scarier than ever as Lady Macbeth, lunged at the audience from the stage. Her blood-stained (well, ketchup- or paint-stained, more likely) palms pressed the air as if it were a wall.

" 'WILL THESE HANDS NE'ER BE CLEAN?' " she shrieked.

"Why doesn't she just go wash them?" Pantelli demanded.

I nodded. "A real weakness in the play."

Beak-Nose was still gesturing. " 'All the perfumes of Arabia will not sweeten this little hand. Oh, *oh*, OH!' "

All this wailing and agonizing became too much for me. I had to confront her, and now, rather than later. Right after the performance we were getting bundled off to a poetry reading.

I crept out of the audience and tiptoed to one side of the auditorium. Except for the stage, where a lone spotlight lit up Mrs. Bridey's ghastly makeup with a weird greenish tinge, the place was pretty dark. I sidled my way between the end seats and the wall to some stairs going up to a curtained area beside the stage.

I pushed through the curtains, only to get lost in the middle of them. Above me, the rings holding the curtain scraped screechingly against the metal rail. "What's that girl doing?" hissed an audience member in the front row.

To heck with it. I wrenched the curtain aside. Clang! The rings came off the bar; a curtain fell on me. More clangs. The loose rings had landed on top of the curtain — on my head, to be exact. Oh well. At least no one could see me now.

Beak-Nose was still wailing out her lines, too involved to have noticed my little scuffle at the side. I leaned forward, not sure what I was going to do except that somehow I had to get her attention.

She cried, " 'To bed, to bed! There's a knocking at the gate — ' "

Clang, clang! The loose curtain rings toppled off my head to the floor.

Beak-Nose hesitated. "Sound effects," I heard her murmur to herself. "I didn't ask for sound effects."

Assuming a tragic expression again, Beak-Nose cried, " 'Come, come, come, come, give me your hand!' "

Was she reciting now? I wasn't sure. Shrugging, I held out my hand, at that moment covered in black curtain.

Beak-Nose and the audience screamed in unison. Too late I realized that my draped hand must have resembled a sinister black blob.

I lifted the folds of curtain so that Beak-Nose, but not the audience, could see who the black blob was.

"Sorry to interrupt," I whispered, "but I'm onto you and this Leo dude."

"Dinah." We were hurrying off to the poetry reading, and Mr. Paigely was beside me. "That strange blob that accosted Lady Macbeth. I happened to notice that you were away from your seat at the time ... "

"Strange blob?" But I was thinking of the even stranger Mrs. Bridey. Her reaction to my, I thought, quite civilized comment had been to turn purple under her white makeup. Her long, beaked nose had trembled; her pinpointy black eyes had blazed. "You get away from me," she'd hissed. "You're nothing, Miss Singing Salami. Do you hear me? NOTHING!"

Her voice had risen on that last word, with the result that murmurs floated from the audience about these puzzling new lines from *Macbeth*.

I'd backed away and slipped off to my seat. What I'd noticed was that Beak-Nose didn't actually deny plotting something.

"Hmmm," I said, narrowing my eyes. Then I remembered that Mr. Paigely was waiting for an answer. "Oh — that blob? It was ... " I didn't like to lie to him. "The blob was ... nothing."

After all, I was only quoting Beak-Nose.

10.
Gotta focus (sigh)

Tap! Tap! Tap! Sl-l-l-l-i-i-ide ... Tap! Tap!

Dancers in black bodysuits and black face paint whirled and glided across the stage. They tiptoed and then kneeled, tiptoed, then kneeled.

A knee creaked.

"Okay!" The assistant director clapped three times, the signal for the dancers to halt. "Somebody want to oil that? This is supposed to be a stealthy routine. You're cat burglars, get it? Not elephant burglars. So not a sound. No creaks. Or burps or hiccups, for that matter."

A cackle from behind me, but that was the stooped, petite cleaning woman, polishing the backs of seats. In front of me, onstage, the dancers started up again. They were playing the shadowy gang of thieves who broke into the mansion and stole Miss Verinder's ring. Tap, tap —

TAP! This last one was my much-chewed pen striking my clipboard in time with the music.

"Dinah," said Jon warningly. "Gotta focus."

His assistant was supervising the dancers. Jon, true to his promise to Ms. Chen, was taking time out to help me with math.

Currently we were struggling through long division. Worse, long division *problems*. "The whole of math is a problem as far as I'm concerned," I wisecracked, but Jon didn't smile.

"You're a smart kid, Dinah," he said. "When I give you directions onstage, you instinctively get what I want you to do, almost even before I've finished saying it. Just like that!" He snapped his fingers. "Whereas I have to explain to the others, even the old pros, a few times at least.

"On the other hand, you've put this barrier up against math when you could quite well get the solutions to it, just as you get my directions. Take down your barrier against math and just let yourself *see* it."

I stared at the numbers before me in my math textbook. They were black and forbidding. I tried to imagine them wriggling free of the problem they were in and arranging themselves into a smiley face.

Then I sighed and tried to concentrate on the problem itself. Gotta focus, I told myself.

Jane's mother has baked 40 pies to bring to a school picnic. There were to be 160 students attending, but 12 have stayed home sick. Jane's mother now has a problem ...

Blah blah blah. I thought of a few choice words I'd like to say to Jane's mother. "Let's see," I sighed. "If there were 160 kids to start out with, then 40 into 160 would be ... um ... "

"Gotta focus," Frank teased, strolling past us down the aisle. He spun and did a mini tap dance on his way down the stairs. "Me, I gotta sing! Gotta dance!" he sang, and I giggled.

And I thought for the thousandth time how very much nicer Frank was than his uncle, the fat-cat producer.

"Hey," I said to Jon, who was wearing a mild frown at the interruption. "Speaking of problems, look what I found."

I pulled the musty scrap of plaid from my pocket and showed it to him.

Jon stared at it. For a second I could have sworn his frown deepened. "Dinah, no offence, but if you're planning to go into the clothes-designing business, you might reconsider. I think your taste in fabric is a bit off."

"*Jon.* This is a clue," I said. Why did adults always have to try to be comedians? They were so

bad at it. "To the mysterious Leo, the jewel thief."
Not wanting to go into details about my scuffle
with Leo, I plunged on. "Have you told Mr.
Murdock there's a plot to steal his moonstone?"

"I did tell him you were concerned." Now Jon
was trying to hide a smile. That was the other annoying thing adults did — act condescending. "Mr.
Murdock went over with me in some detail all the
protective measures he was taking, with security
guards and so on."

"But when I challenged Beak-Nose, she practi-
cally admitted — at least, she didn't deny — "

"Violet Bridey isn't even in town," Jon said
firmly. "She moved back east a couple of days ago.
She's *gone*, Dinah."

11.
Dinah and Madge go eavesdropping

"Yup." Jon grinned. " 'Beak-Nose,' as you unkindly call her, sent a scornful farewell e-mail to me and various other members of our local theater community. She maintained that Vancouver didn't appreciate her."

I didn't get it. Beak-Nose would have to be around on opening night to help the mysterious Leo swipe the moonstone. She couldn't be back east for that.

I sighed in time with the *whish*! of the cleaning woman's broom nearby. Gray and stooped, she cackled out a "Thank 'ee, dearie," as I lifted my feet for her to sweep underneath.

If only I could clear the dust out of my brain. Like, to figure out who the mysterious Leo was. Since I didn't know, I could only imagine him with the vaguest features, the way I'd imagined eyes, nose and a mouth in the moonstone ring Cindi had flashed around the other night.

That's what I had to figure out: who the man in the moonstone was.

Jon left me to deal with Jane and her pies while he went off to a meeting with Mr. Murdock. The fat producer had blustered in, red and sweaty, and demanded to talk about certain "concerns." Poor Jon. I knew he was already stressed about getting all of us ready for opening night without being nagged at.

I grappled with Jane's pie problem until the exercise book was grimy with rubbed-out numbers that had been written over and then rubbed out again. Hmmm. Maybe a series of arrows would help. I drew long, winding ones to show Jon the path of my, er, calculations.

Then, clutching the exercise book, I marched proudly up the aisle to the lobby. Mr. Murdock liked meeting Jon there because that's where the vending machines were. (I couldn't fault him for that.) I was sure Jon wouldn't mind a break from Mr. Murdock's nagging while I showed him my work.

Ker-runch! The producer was chomping his way through a bag of barbecue-flavored corn chips. A lot of the chips' orange powder gleamed on his red cheeks.

"The kid's gotta go," he boomed at Jon.

I stopped and ducked back into the doorway.

"Dinah's perfect for the part," Jon objected, looking tired. "She's got heart. She's got energy. And," his slim features glimmered with a smile, "she's got a contract."

Mr. Murdock scrounged in the chip bag for crumbs. "I liked the other kid. Y'know, the dainty one. Angela what's-her-face."

"Coretta isn't a dainty character, sir. She's more — well, the speeding-locomotive type, let's say."

The producer's doughy forehead sank into several layers of frowns. "Don't joke with me, Horowitz." He jabbed orangey fingertips at Jon. "I don't like jokes."

Then, with smacking noises, he licked each fingertip.

Frank got that angry look that made him extra handsome. "You mean Jon just *sat* there when my uncle bad-mouthed you?"

"Oh no, he defended me," I said. "And then, after, Jon was really nice to me when he corrected my math and found it to be," I paused sadly, "all wrong. I guess he was feeling bad that Mr. Murdock doesn't like me."

Frank calmed down and managed a grin. "Well,

okay. I guess I know my uncle rather too well. This is typically rotten of him. Typically interfering. If I'd been Jon, I would've punched him."

"Ooo, Frank," gushed Cindi. "You wouldn't!" She let out a thrilled mini-shriek.

We were waiting at one side of the stage, in the "wings," as it's called, to rehearse a scene.

"What I don't get is why Mr. Murdock wants me out of the show," I mused. "Just like Beak-Nose and Leo do, I mean. It's as if ... "

As if Mr. Murdock were in on whatever they were plotting. Hey, maybe *he* was Leo. He was sure fat enough. And he had gray hair, albeit with a pink bald patch at the back of his head.

But why would he want to steal his own moonstone?

Thunk!

Trying to parallel park, Madge had bumped the rear fender of our family car, an old, die-hard Toyota Tercel, against the front of a sleek, shining Infiniti convertible.

"Madge," I said uneasily. "Maybe we should find a place that's more suited to your parking skills. Like a wide open field."

"That's enough, Dinah," my sister snapped. "If this idiot behind me had just left me a bit more room — " *Thunk!* "There, I think that's got it."

We were near Kitsilano Beach. Mother and Jon were having dinner at a Vietnamese restaurant, Saigon Bliss. Madge, very *un*blissed about their budding relationship, wanted to check up on them.

We got out of the car. The front of it was jutting out at an odd angle onto the street. Even though I was bad at math concepts, I was pretty sure this wasn't what "parallel" meant.

Madge took my hand to cross the street. "I just have a bad feeling about Mother and Jon," she worried. "I mean, he's *younger* than she is, Dinah. Sooner or later, he'll decide he wants some twenty-year-old bimbo. These showbiz types always do. Every time you pick up *People* magazine, you read about it."

"I SAW THAT!"

A teenaged boy in a leather jacket ran towards us. "I SAW YOU NICK MY DAD'S INFINITI!" He reached us, panting.

"I haven't *nicked* anything of anyone's," Madge said scornfully. "If he'd park properly, other people wouldn't have to struggle to get in ahead of him."

"If *he'd* — Listen, I've a good mind to report you to ... "

The boy stopped. Somewhere in the middle of

his indignation he'd got a look at Madge.

" — to ... to ... " His voice petered out. A soft, silly expression settled on his face. "Gosh. Would you like to go out sometime?"

As I've noted before, this type of thing happens a lot with my sister. We were so used to it that we simply walked away and forgot about the boy. He'd recover, in time.

Mixed scents of peanut sauce, garlic, peppery hot and sour soup, and black bean sauce poured out of Saigon Bliss's windows. I'd been there before with Mother and Madge. No matter what the weather, Saigon Bliss kept its windows open because of the steam and hot, sizzling spices that charged every which way from the kitchen.

Madge gripped my hand. "Look! There's Mother and Jon!" she whispered.

They were chatting at a table by one of the windows. Jon had removed his glasses and set them beside his place mat, probably because they were steaming up from the chef's energetic cooking.

"Let's go join Mother and Jon," I suggested. "I could use a post-dinner snack."

"That would defeat our whole purpose," she scolded.

"Um, what exactly *is* our purpose?"

"To find out what he's up to, of course. To protect Mother from heartbreak."

A hedge separated the sidewalk from the restaurant. Ducking, Madge pulled me behind the hedge and below window level until we were alongside Mother and Jon's table.

We knelt. The spicy scents were agonizingly strong, and my stomach began to grumble.

"Ssshhh!" hissed Madge.

"I can't control it," I retorted, hurt. "Madge, you've heard of the falling stock market. How 'bout the *falling I.Q.*? This is the dumbest situation you've ever — "

"WILL YOU BE QUIET!" Realizing she'd raised her voice, Madge clapped a hand over her mouth.

She was crouching next to Jon's side of the window. As a result, we heard him say, bewildered, to Mother, "Am I disturbing you?" Unable to see well without his glasses, he must've assumed it was her voice he'd heard.

"Not at all," Mother assured him. "If I'm wincing, it's because of the soup being so spicy. But I am enjoying it, truly!"

"Oh yeah?" he teased. "Well, I find you very disturbing, Suzanne. As in, you disturb my thoughts almost every hour."

"Oh *no*," groaned Madge.

"Oh yes," Jon told Mother. "But I won't mention it again if I'm making you uncomfortable."

I myself was getting uncomfortable — from hunger. Meanwhile, Mother was prevented from replying by the arrival of the waiter. "Your spring rolls, Madame and Sir! And may I show you the wine list?"

Spring rolls! I couldn't stand it. Ignoring Madge's frantic signals to stay put, I got up and peered over the windowsill.

Mother and Jon were occupied with browsing the wine menu that the waiter was holding open. He was pointing out different wines to them.

Right in front of me sat Mother's plate, with two large, prawn-stuffed spring rolls, and peanut sauce in a paper cup.

I reached in, grabbed the rolls and the peanut sauce, and withdrew them out the window.

"A chilled chardonnay, I think," Jon said to the waiter.

"Are you insane?" Madge squeaked at me.

Jon asked Mother in surprise, "Why, would you prefer a red wine, Suzanne?"

"Oh, I much prefer white," said Mother. "Red wine gives me headaches."

"Uh ... " Jon sounded confused. "Okay. White it is."

My curiosity was too much for me. (Like it ever wasn't.) I peeked over the sill. With a bow, the waiter was retreating; Jon had turned back to Mother.

"Hey," he exclaimed, noticing her empty plate. "Y'know, I like a woman with an appetite. I know so many actresses who starve themselves to thinness. You're really refreshing ... Wow, and the paper cup, too!"

" ... so you see," Mother was telling Jon, "Dinah has got over her dad's death better than Madge, perhaps because Dinah is younger and more resilient. Madge is very loyal to her father's memory. She's also very sensitive — you can see that in her drawings and paintings. It was only this past summer that she could even start talking about her father. That was thanks to the young man in her life, Jack French. He's back east right now.

"Anyhow, I'm just trying to say — " Mother hesitated.

"That we should take it easy," Jon finished gently for her. "Okay by me, Suzanne. I can understand that not only you, but also the girls, need to get used to me.

"I haven't got to know Madge yet, but from what Dinah's said, it sounds like your late husband taught the girls a lot about music. All I have to do is mention an old standard by Frank Sinatra or Dean Martin, and Dinah can belt out all the lyrics."

"Dinah's wonderful that way," Mother said fondly. "She's got so much love and energy."

Wow. I was just developing a warm glow at this praise when Mother went on.

"If only she'd apply some of her energy to math! I know she could do well if she wanted to."

Jon said something irritating about working on math with me, and then Mother offered to invite him over for dinner. "We have a huge collection of Frank's and Dean's music," she said.

Madge whispered to me indignantly, "That was Dad's collection!"

"Really — your father's?" Jon asked Mother, impressed. "Genuine, original record albums, then!"

"Heavens, no," Mother said. "Just CDs."

"But I thought you said — huh." Jon paused, bewildered again. "Anyhow, I particularly like Dean's stuff. "'That's Amore', for instance. Or, 'Ain't That A Kick in the Head.'"

Madge bumped our old family Toyota against the Infiniti and then took off with a squeal of tires.

She glanced at me. "Dinah, your mouth has

been hanging open for the past five minutes. Maybe I should put some birdseed on your tongue and we can put you in the garden to use as a feeder."

I glared back at her. "Leave the jokes to other people, Madge. Humor isn't your strong point."

She giggled, apparently not believing me. I blamed Jack. He encouraged Madge by laughing uproariously at her lame wisecracks. Teens in love: *honestly*.

Then Madge sighed. "But what to do about Mother! The woman is so naïve."

My sister embarked on a long lecture about older women being attracted to younger men, when it was guys their own age they should go for. I'd read the original of this lecture in one of Madge's magazines, so I tuned it out.

Tune was the operative word. Specifically, the tune "Ain't That A Kick in the Head." One of Jon's favorite songs — and an expression the mysterious Leo used all the time.

Well, Jon couldn't *be* Leo. The sad-faced young man in the café had described Leo as fat. Jon was slim.

But maybe Leo and Jon hung out together. Maybe they were buddies.

Maybe — my mouth plopped open again — they were thick as thieves.

12.
Behind the closet door

The next morning Mr. Paigely gave us back the most recent math test. I'd managed a C+. I was improving, but on straight equations, not problems. They still baffled me. *Don't hesitate to ask me if you need help*, Mr. Paigely had written in the margin.

I picked up a pen and chewed on it. I needed help all right.

"Uh, that's *my* pen," Pantelli objected. Grabbing it, he scowled at the fresh teeth marks on the end.

Oops. Oh, well, in my opinion, teeth marks added character to a pen. I put my hand up. "Mr. Paigely, why would somebody be in a plot to steal his own valuables?"

Mr. Paigely goggled at me. (Well, he'd *said* I could ask him for help.) "Hmm." He considered, and then brightened. "To collect insurance?"

"Hey," I said. "Good one."

"Do I get an A?" joked Mr. Paigely.

A feeble joke, but we laughed anyhow. These days we were laughing with him, not at him. Yup, we'd decided Mr. Paigely was all right.

That afternoon, in rehearsal of the "Blue Moon" number, Jon praised me in front of everyone for putting more emotion into my singing. "You're right to tone down the volume a bit sometimes. With those softer notes, you make us feel how much Coretta misses her dad, far away in India," he said.

I shrugged, as if the compliment didn't mean much to me. After all, a kid has to appear cool, right? But of course it did mean a lot. The reason I was sounding more emotional was that I thought of my own dad when I sang. He, too, was far away. Permanently far away.

Then Jon started working with Cindi, to tone down the screams that were still slipping into *her* part of "Blue Moon."

Frank and I headed to the snack machine in the lobby. "I think Jon's all wrong to want your volume toned down," he confided to me. "When you belt 'em out, people get chills up their spine."

I broke into a pleased grin, but before I could

say anything, a loud trumpeting filled the lobby.

Cindi, blowing her nose. "Oh, Frank! Jon's so m-m-mean! He says I've got to stop sounding like a fire engine when I sing!"

Sobbing, she rushed into his arms. "There, there," Frank soothed and kissed the tip of her nose.

Oh, brother. "Pardon me," I said pointedly. "I, at least, have *work* to tend to. Investigative work." I marched off.

Heading downstairs, I made my footsteps less of a march, more of a tiptoe. I'd decided to investigate Jon's office. He'd stood up for me with Mr. Murdock, but I was still suspicious of him.

His office, along with the changing rooms, was underneath the theater's main level. There was another level even below that, with the furnace room and other utility and storage space, but this lower level was off-limits to all except the janitors.

The dancers who played the thieves were in the big changing room. "Yo, Dinah!" one of them called. Normally I liked chatting with the dancers. Throughout any conversation they kept doing pliés and deep knee bends. But right now I didn't much want to be noticed. I edged past to Jon's office, at the end of the hall and just before the stairs down to the forbidden level. I slipped into his office and shut the door.

Five minutes later I'd found nothing but actor contracts and stage directions. I knew I should be getting back upstairs. It was about time for me to rehearse the scene where I, as Coretta Cuff, sneak into the kitchen for a midnight snack, only to discover Frank, as Miss Verinder's fiancé, sleepwalking.

I hoped Frank wouldn't make me giggle, as he had at the previous rehearsal of that scene. Stretching out his arms, he'd waggled his fingers at me and pretended to stalk towards me like Frankenstein. Jon had not been impressed.

I stacked all Jon's papers up more or less the way they'd been. Then trudging round his desk to the door, I was suddenly wrenched back.

A closet doorknob had snared one of the buttonholes on my sweater. As I pulled the sweater loose, the closet door came open.

There were tons of costumes inside, from ballgowns to clown outfits. "Cool," I breathed, pawing through them. I hoped some day I could wear a funky clown costume, complete with face paint. In *The Moonstone* I was stuck with frilly dresses and, get this, *extra* freckles pasted on. As if I didn't have enough natural ones.

I rummaged farther. Hey, a pink tuxedo. And

a black stovepipe hat! And a gi-normous, shabby, orange-and-green plaid jacket with built-in padding, and —

Wait just a minute.

I pushed the other outfits aside and stared at the plaid jacket. A pocket was missing. The pocket I'd torn off.

And, whoa — a gray wig was crammed into the other pocket. The gray hair I'd assumed was Leo's own.

Also, the padding meant that Leo himself wasn't necessarily fat. He'd just dressed up to look that way.

A chill came over me that even my woolly sweater couldn't warm. All at once I thrust the other outfits back against the jacket. Then I backed away, half-expecting it to raise one armless sleeve and yank me deep into the closet's musty depths. And to croon, while it was doing so, "Ain't That A Kick In The Head."

I retreated into the hall and shut the office door against the sight of that jacket and wig. It was impossible to shut out what I was realizing, though.

Jon was Leo.

13.
More tricks than treats

The moon had thinned. It quivered between the wisps of clouds like a dangly earring.

Huh, I thought, disappointed. Halloween night, and only a crescent moon.

The moon wasn't all I was annoyed with. I scrambled round on the bay window seat of our living room to see Jon examining our jack-o'-lantern. Madge and I had carved out a particularly strange face this year: madly sloping mouth, gory gashes in the cheeks, and an eyeball from the party favors store hanging by a spring from one socket.

"Handsome devil," commented Jon, amused.

I scowled at him, not that he'd be able to tell, with the emerald green witch's makeup slathered all over my face. I would be trick-or-treating after dinner.

Which, to Madge's and my dismay, Mother had invited him to.

"What's the jack-o'-lantern's name?" Jon inquired.

"It's *Leo*," I responded fiercely, then plucked up the black folds of my witch's cape and skirt and fled into the dining room.

Madge was setting out plates, each with a cling-on skeleton hand. Fake cobwebs hung from our otherwise dignified old brass-and-etched-glass chandelier. A crystal bowl brimmed with tiny black plastic spiders.

Let's just say that, in our household, we take our seasonal themes seriously.

In the center of the table, a bowl held Madge's lovely arrangement of red and gold leaves. Madge was amazing. She could take stuff you'd find sprouting in the yard or drifting over the sidewalk and transform it into art.

"Jon is a criminal," I informed her over the salad. To emphasize my point, I removed a radish and crunched it with maximum ear-splitting effect.

"Exactly. Preying on older women like this," Madge agreed darkly. Pouring out a dollop of Mother's lemony mustard dressing from a pitcher, she grabbed the tongs and tossed the salad with angry vigor.

"Isn't this nice," said Mother a short while later, as we were sitting round the table. "Madge helped me make this squash, Jon. It's got cinnamon and brown sugar in it, and of course hugely unhealthy amounts of butter." She passed him the casserole dish.

"Looks and smells wonderful," smiled Jon.

Madge gave a thin smile. "Oh, Jon probably regards this type of dish as quaint, Mother. Old-fashioned. You know, *from a previous generation.*"

"Uh ... " Jon gazed at her in bewilderment. He opened his mouth to protest, but I got there ahead of him.

"Better watch it, Madge. You might end up locked in a washroom."

Ha! That showed Jon I was onto him. Pleased with myself, I poured extra gravy on my mashed potatoes until they were submerged. "I call this the sinking of Atlantis," I explained to the other three.

The washroom reference hadn't meant anything to Madge — in fact, it was puzzling enough to have silenced both her and Mother.

But not for long. Madge chirped up brightly, "Gosh, the city of Atlantis! That sank ages ago — in your childhood, I guess, Mother."

"I'm certainly getting a sinking feeling now," Mother remarked, glancing from Madge to me. "Is something wrong, girls?"

In response, Madge burst into tears. I jammed

my pointy witch's hat farther down on my head and glared at her. Trust Madge to go all girlish. Some colleague she was.

To punish her for wimping out, I said sweetly, "So Jack's still not back! Maybe he's met some nice Eastern gal."

"Dinah!" exclaimed Mother, shocked.

I began to eat very rapidly. It was just a matter of time before I'd be sent from the table. No time to cut up this nummy, tender white turkey: just slather on cranberry sauce, fold the turkey over it — instant sandwich! — and tuck it back.

I used fingers, of course. A complicated maneuver like that couldn't be left to knife and fork.

"Dinah!" repeated Mother. Jon just stared.

Well, I'd give him something to stare at. I began rotating my arms in imitation of a windmill. As in Windmill Café. Clever, huh?

"That does it," said Mother. "Off you go."

I pushed my chair under the table and departed. As often happened, I hadn't made it through to dessert.

That night it didn't matter, though. It was Halloween! Lots of candies in store.

"Ya ready, Di?" Pantelli bellowed up to my window. Pantelli rarely bothered with doorbells.

Lifting my witch's skirt for easier running, I escaped down the stairs and outside before Mother could think of objecting. She might ground me from going out on Halloween: I had been, as I was fond of saying, at the top of my form during dinner.

Pantelli's dad accompanied us. "Wooo-wooo, Dinah," he pretend-shuddered. Luckily he soon got into conversation with another dad making the rounds with other kids, so I didn't have to put up with any more of his silliness.

"By the way, one of the jewel thieves is in my house right now," I confided to Pantelli as we loaded up at the Ungerleiders'.

"No way!" Pantelli's brown-painted face gaped at me from beneath his huge straw hat, pasted all over with leaves. He was, needless to say, trick-or-treating as a tree. "You mean, the thief's in your house *stealing*?"

"Don't be ridiculous. He's eating there."

We paused to yell, "SHELL OUT, SHELL OUT, THE WITCHES ARE OUT!" at the Chens'. Yeah, Chen, as in the principal of Lord Bithersby.

"Oh, hello, Dinah, Pantelli," Ms. Chen greeted us. "Ah! A tree again this year, Pantelli. Great makeup jobs, both of you."

"Madge did our makeup," I explained, respecting Ms. Chen for not faking a cringe or

wooo-wooo-ing at the sight of us. I held my goody
bag wide for my very favorite treat, peanut butter-
filled chocolates. Ultra-num. Ms. Chen was pretty
nice, for a principal. Every year she remembered
that I liked them.

"How's the math tutoring going, Dinah?" she
inquired.

"That's too ghoulish a question, Ms. Chen."

She laughed. "All right, you two. Watch your
step tonight: there's not much of a moon."

We looked up. The silver earring was being
swallowed up by a gray cloud. In my mind I saw
again the Murdock moonstone on Cindi's finger,
just as silver and creamy as that wisp in the sky.

I imagined the ring similarly fading, till there
was nothing left on Cindi's hand. Which would
happen, if thieves struck.

I shuddered, and not a pretend one, either.

"Listen," I said to Pantelli as we accepted tan-
gerines from the McGillicuddys, who refused to
give out sweets, "how good a look did you get at
Leo? When you were up in the tree beside Mrs.
Bridey's apartment, I mean. He wouldn't have been
in disguise then."

"Uh," said Pantelli, inspecting his tangerine with
disappointment. "An okay look I guess."

"C'mon, you two," complained Mrs.

McGillicuddy. "Whatever happened to 'Trick or Treat' and other Halloween sayings? Tradition, children! Customs!"

"TRICK OR TREAT!" we yelled obligingly.

Three streets later I had an idea. "We'll sneak a peek at Jon," I told Pantelli. "You can tell me if he's the guy you saw through Mrs. Bridey's window ... oh, Mr. Audia," I called to Pantelli's dad on the sidewalk, "we want to go back to my place for a break."

"A *break*? On Halloween? Are you feeling ill, Dinah?"

And Pantelli protested, "We can't afford to lose time, not on Halloween." He showed me the contents of his bag. "Barely a quarter full, Di."

"Pantelli, anyone who goes out with a *duffel* bag — "

"Okay, okay. A fast sneak peek, though."

"I'll be back soon," Mr. Audia said when he'd walked us back to my place. "The fireworks will be starting soon, and I'm sure you don't want to take a break from them."

Every Halloween the neighbors get together to blaze fireworks in a starry shower down our steep hill. It's something we always look forward to, but tonight, business first.

I peeked through the front door's glass pane. The glass sure had lots of smudges — oh, wait. That was my breath coming out in clouds.

I saw a fire glowing in the fireplace. In front of it basked Wilfred, tummy up and fluffed out.

Mother and Jon were sitting on the sofa, drinking coffee and talking. The only trouble was, their backs were to us.

"We'll have to sneak round the back of the Dubuques' for you to see him," I told Pantelli. I gave up trying to look through the door. Every time I got things into focus, a breath cloud would block my view.

"Huh? Why can't we just go in?" Pantelli's leaf-laden forehead pressed against the glass pane. When he removed it, several of the leaves had come off and stuck to the glass.

"I don't want to tip Jon off that I have a witness. C'mon, we can spy on him from the Dubuques' deck."

We hid our loot bags behind one of Mother's huge planters. Then, grumbling, Pantelli followed me along the path beside the Dubuques' house.

One thing I should explain about Mr. and Mrs. Dubuque. Not being fond of kids, they don't believe in shelling out on Halloween. So, every October 31, they pull their blinds firmly down and watch TV behind them.

Which meant the path alongside their house was inky dark. "Ow!" yelped Pantelli, tripping over something that clanged down the walk ahead of us. It gleamed in the pale sliver of moonlight: a watering can.

Upstairs, a light went on in a side window. Scr-r-reech! The window shot up. Pantelli and I froze. "What was that, Albert?' asked Mrs. Dubuque.

Her husband grunted, right above us, "Musta been a raccoon ... Hey, Lou, lookit."

"Yes, Albert?"

I froze against the wall, hoping my witch outfit would blend into the shadows. Not much could be done about Pantelli, though. The light from the window danced against the leaves of his hat. Uh-oh. "Be prepared to run," I hissed.

"Ya oughtta prune the bushes, Lou. They're taking over the path."

The window slammed down.

Clasping the rails of the Dubuques' deck, we swung up and over. Crash! Pantelli landed on a patio chair — which promptly collapsed with deafening creaks and rattles.

Lights went on in the Dubuques' dining room, which was right beside the deck. Pantelli and I leaped back over the railing. I ended up on the inky-shadowy path at the side of the house. Pantelli dropped into the back yard and started to run across various flowerbeds to the back gate.

Too late. The glass doors slid open and Mr. and Mrs. Dubuque stepped out on the deck.

14.
Hold it. A nice thief?

Pantelli crouched in the middle of a flowerbed. The Dubuques didn't switch on the outside light; with any luck they wouldn't notice him.

I pressed myself against the side of the house and fervently hoped they'd go back in soon.

"Such a lovely night, Albert," sighed Mrs. Dubuque. "Those clouds drifting across the sky ... that wisp of a moon ... "

"It'll be a lovely night when those noisy kids go home, Lou. Banging on doors! Yelling! Making nuisances of themselves! Well, we outfoxed 'em all right, Lou. Little do the pests suspect we're out back, savoring the tranquility of our own garden."

Just then the wisp of moon struggled out from behind the clouds to illuminate the Dubuques' garden — including the newest addition to one of their flowerbeds.

"Albert, there's a strange plant over there. Did you put in a new shrub? I must say, it's not a very attractive one."

"Huh? What — hey, I see what you mean. Ugly as all get-out, isn't it? Must be a weed," Mr. Dubuque said indignantly. "Well, I'll just get me some shears and chop it up."

I gulped. If they thought this new plant looked strange now, wait till they saw it stand up and run away.

"Albert! It's — *it's moving!*"

Pantelli sprinted to their back gate and let himself out. I forgot to be nervous and let out a low snort of laughter.

"What was that?" Mrs. Dubuque demanded.

"Could be a raccoon."

"No way I'm tackling a raccoon with my bare hands, Lou. I'll get me a shovel and bash it out, the lazy fat critter. Bet it's the one that's been breaking into our garbage cans, the greedy, slothful — "

"Be careful, Albert! It might bite!"

"It" was actually much more scared of them, if they only knew. I ran, accidentally kicking the watering can again.

"I hear the thieving raccoon — it's at the side!" roared Mr. Dubuque.

With his footsteps thudding after me, I stumbled into the shelter of my front yard.

And, in a desperate effort to disguise my true identity, I let out a long, agonized wolf howl.

Feeling quite pleased with the howl, I met up with Pantelli under the streetlamp at the corner. Night or day, this was our rendezvous point after escapes from wrathful neighbors. Of whom, it has to be admitted, Mr. Dubuque was the most frequent.

"That was one lame attempt to sound like a wolf," Pantelli greeted me. He handed over my loot bag, which he'd retrieved, along with his own, from behind Mother's planter.

I didn't have time to feel offended by Pantelli's comment, even though *I* thought my wolf imitation had been very skilful.

More to the point, Pantelli hadn't had a chance to look at Jon. Dang it. I had to arrange an opportunity somehow.

Mr. Audia, strolling down the sidewalk, waved his hand at us. In the sparse moonlight he seemed to have sprouted a sixth finger; under the lamp we saw it was a Tootsie Roll.

"Fireworks are starting," Mr. Audia told us. He took a bite of Tootsie Roll so that his teeth stuck together and made his next remark inaudible, but we assumed it was, "Let's go."

So, we went. Blue, gold, green and red fireworks scooted all over the sky. The littler kids opened their loot bags to try and catch them.

After a while, a different type of fireworks erupted behind us. "I tell you, it was a fat, hulking raccoon," Mr. Dubuque exploded to Mr. Audia.

I glanced down at my witchly-outfitted self. Pudgy, yes, but I didn't think I was fat. Okay, I'd eliminate dill-pickle-flavored potato chips. And winegums. That was it, though.

"It could have been just a fat rat," Mr. Audia was suggesting.

Beside me, Pantelli muffled a long, rude laugh with his hand.

When I got home, Madge announced to me radiantly: "Jack phoned. He's coming home!"

I cheered. My "How well do you communicate with your boyfriend?" survey had paid off. Yet another Dinah-mite triumph.

Madge went on, "Jack was planning to stay a month longer with his family, but he said he's worried about me losing interest in him. Can you imagine?"

I could well imagine. I put on what I hoped was a puzzled smile.

"You don't have a toothache, do you, Dinah?"

Madge inquired in sudden concern. She hugged me again. "Hey, Mother, you're being awfully subdued. Are you okay?"

"Yes, dear," Mother said, managing a smile. The doorbell blared several times with more trick-or-treaters, and she went to open the door.

"She's thinking about Jon," Madge murmured, with a stricken look. "Or the lack of Jon, I mean. He's left. Mother told him we weren't ready for her to see anyone else. You know, romantically." Madge sighed. "Now it seems kind of unfair, me getting my boyfriend back, and Mother having to give up hers."

"Maybe we did go overboard in the way we treated Jon at dinner," I whispered back. "We *were* pretty awful."

I felt worse and worse. After all, if Mother liked the guy ... On the other hand, he was most likely a jewel thief.

Mother passed us with her quiet smile. In the dining room, she began collecting the dirty dishes. I'd seen her do this a zillion times, yet all at once, this particular night, she appeared so very alone in there.

I changed into some dry clothes and, in a first, helped Mother clean up without being asked.

Madge was helping, too, and looking just as solemn as I felt. She must've also noticed Mother's aloneness, because we exchanged guilty looks over her leaves-and-flowers arrangement. Different as Madge and I were, we were sisters, and we knew what each other was thinking: that Mother liked Jon, and we'd driven him away.

"But he's a crook," I rationalized to the moon.

I was sitting on my window seat. The window was the old-fashioned kind, with two panes that opened sideways, like doors. There was a crabapple tree right outside, mostly bare now. Through its branches I was watching the moon, or what there was of it. If I let out too big a breath I might blow it out.

"He's a would-be thief," I added.

However, much as I believed Jon and the mysterious Leo were one and the same, it wasn't the criminal side of Jon that I was able to concentrate on. I kept remembering how nice he'd been a few days before, during a rehearsal.

This rehearsal was a dress one. Which meant that, in addition to frills and ruffles, I had to wear contact lenses: Coretta Cuff wasn't supposed to be bespectacled.

I hated the contacts. They made me blink horribly. My eyes were always full of water.

As we began my first scene, I stumbled against

a sofa. Miss Verinder (Cindi) had been lying there in a dead faint; when I bumped against her, she sat up in surprise.

There was a cackle from the cleaning woman, whishing her broom around between audience seats.

"Okay, Dinah," sighed Jon. "Listen. I know how you feel. I myself tried contact lenses once, and my eyes poured tears like the falls at Capilano Dam. How 'bout if I let you wear glasses for every rehearsal? Do you think you could memorize your movements so well that you wouldn't have to wear your glasses when we open?"

"You bet," I said in relief. "I've got my house memorized in just that way. You know, for when I come down to breakfast with my eyes shut. It's a technique I use for getting a few extra minutes of half-sleep, if you know what I mean."

"Right," said Jon, and — *cackle!* The cleaning woman chortled again.

So everything turned out fine. I didn't have to wear contacts. But now, as I regarded the wisp of a moon, my eyes were watering even without them.

The moon blurred. Wiping my eyes with the back of my hand, I asked it, "What should I do? Jon's been nice to me. And I know Mother likes him."

The moon bobbed over the mountains like an

apostrophe separated from the rest of its sentence. "I can't possibly hold a conversation with you when you're looking like that," I told it sternly.

"What's wrong with the way I look?" Madge demanded behind me.

She joined me on the window seat. Naturally, her question had been rhetorical. Madge knew quite well how pretty she looked, with her dark red hair, freshly washed with honey shampoo, in a cloud around her porcelain complexion, freshly softened with vanilla cream. With the cosmetics Madge bought, I never knew how she figured out whether to apply them or eat them.

She said, "I have a feeling our minds are in synch" — and then she paused to grimace. "From my point of view, a frightening thought, but no matter. What I mean is, we should give Jon another chance, shouldn't we?"

"Um." I tapped several nail-chomped fingers on the windowsill. Even if Jon went to jail, which crooks eventually do, he and Mother could at least send romantic e-mails to each other. It'd be something.

"Okay," I said, in sudden decision. "But we'll have to let Mother and Jon know that it's all right with us. Subtly, of course." I brightened. "Hey. We'll fill out one of those magazine love surveys on

Mother's behalf and mail it to Jon."

Madge rolled her eyes. "How ridiculous, Dinah! As if anyone wouldn't see through a ploy like *that*!"

15.
Problems, problems

At school the next morning we had one of those baffling math tests with problems about people having to divide things up.

For ages I gnawed the end of my pen over the problem of a moron named Tom, who'd brought too few hockey sticks to a tournament. Finally, when the bell blared and I'd got no closer to solving Tom's goof-up, I scribbled a note to Mr. Paigely at the bottom of the test:

If this dweeb had learned his math properly, he would've brought the right amount of hockey sticks to begin with, right?

I set down the by-now badly deformed pen and permitted myself a thin, triumphant smile. That'd show Paigely!

However, it didn't. He saw the note as he collected my paper and chuckled. "Dinah, your difficulty is that you're not getting *inside* these problems," Mr. Paigely informed me, with the happy, dreamy smile that came over him whenever he explained a concept.

"Instead, you've adopted a lofty view of the problems. From on high, as it were," he went on, confusing me utterly. "You're seeing each problem as a whole and dismissing it as too bewildering. What you need to do is get involved with what matters and push the other stuff aside."

He wandered off humming, oblivious to the scowl I sent after him. Get involved with math, indeed! Our regular teacher, Ms. LaFontaine, would've read my note, sniffed with indignation and dispatched me to the principal's office straightaway.

I tell you, I almost missed her.

The rest of the afternoon looked to be much more productive. My class was off to visit the Livingston Theater for a tour, plus watching a dress rehearsal. We were all going in the school bus, after lunch.

Which meant Pantelli would have a chance to see Jon. To identify him, or not, as the guy in Beak-Nose's window.

In the bus I dozed off. I went to sleep with my nose scrunched up because I was sitting next to Lee Ann Hornblower, a large, wispy-beige-haired girl known for her b.o. It was in full force that day and, unfortunately, it was also in the dream I had while the school bus rattled along.

"This is bad enough in my waking hours," I complained to Lee Ann. *"Do you have to ruin my naps as well?"*

She beamed at me. Stupid cow, I thought.

"Mooooo," she said.

The appearance of Frank Murdock in the seat ahead of me was a relief. Not really a surprise, because this was a dream. "Could you please find me another seat?" I asked him.

Cindi Kahn materialized beside Frank. "Oh, Frank can do anything," she assured me, fixing him with a worshipful gaze.

I would've done the same thing, because I liked Frank a lot myself, but I couldn't unscrunch my nose. "Please," I begged Frank.

Frank smiled apologetically. "I can't. It wouldn't be nice."

He winked at me, then evaporated. Bit by bit, jigsaw-puzzle style, the person who materialized in his place was — Jon! "This 'nice' stuff," he tsked, shaking his head at me. "The play's the thing. You have to focus, Dinah, or you'll never put feeling into your voice."

"Or emotion into your acting," nodded Cindi.

"Or understanding into your math," put in Mr. Paigely, passing by.

I shrugged at Jon. "I'm stumped. Are you Leo, or aren't you?"

"Oh, well, as to that," he chuckled. Piece by jigsaw piece, he began to transform into a bulky orange-and-green plaid jacket topped by a mop of gray hair. The face was in shadows, but I knew who it had to be — Leo.

Leo's big, tweedy arms reached for me.

"HELP," I shouted. But, being a dream, the shout only came out as: "HELP!"

"Focus, Dinah," Mr. Paigely called.

I tried struggling out of the seat. Useless. My body was leaden.

"Do something," I begged Cindi, who, to one side of Leo, was growing more and more goggly-eyed at my predicament.

Obligingly, she began to scream. And SCREAM.

I woke up. The whole bus was in an uproar, kids yelling and shrieking. Holding my nose, I leaned close to Lee Ann. "Whad is id?" I demanded. "Whad is goink od?" I didn't want to be rude to people — every few weeks Mother gave me a long, long talk about this, but Lee Ann's b.o. was so strong that day I couldn't help it.

Fortunately, she was so busy shrieking herself that she didn't notice. "Pantelli threw up," she paused to inform me with great gusto. "He stuck his head out the window and heaved. Got a pedestrian on the shoulder."

I got up on my seat and looked round for Pantelli. There he was, being consoled by Mr. Paigely. Our regular teacher knew Pantelli got motion sickness on buses; she always arranged for one of his parents or a volunteer to drive him on field trips. Knowing Pantelli, I was pretty sure he'd been too embarrassed to tell Mr. Paigely about his problem with heaving. He'd tried to be the strong, silent type. What a doofus.

Pantelli saw me grimacing at him and scowled. Trying to cheer him up, I yelled, "A pedestrian! Good aim, buddy!" Positive reinforcement is *so* important, I believe.

I settled back into my seat. Too bad I hadn't been sitting beside Pantelli. *I* wouldn't have shrieked when he'd barfed out the window, and no one else would have noticed.

Except for the pedestrian, of course.

But stinky Lee Ann had prevented that. She'd sandwiched herself in beside me before he could. All because we went to the same church and our mothers thought it would be nice if we became friends.

Nice! There was that word again.

I held my nose and didn't care if I offended Lee Ann or not.

On arriving at the theater, Mr. Paigely took Pantelli into the front office to drink big glassfuls of water. "But I'm fine now!" Pantelli objected. "C'mon, Mr. Paigely: making me drink water! Don't you think that's going a bit far?"

Then Cindi, who was hovering nearby, made him a large pot of peppermint tea. Poor Pantelli!

I slipped in to visit him while Jon took the rest of the class on a tour through the theater. Cindi and Mr. Paigely were busy discussing the merits of herbal versus fruit-flavored tea — *fun* — so I was able to ask Pantelli, "Well? Is he the guy you saw through Beak-Nose's window?"

Pantelli gazed thoughtfully at Mr. Paigely. "Gee, I don't think so."

"No!" I clutched my hair. Someday I would actually start ripping it out. "I mean *Jon.*"

"Oh." Pantelli shrugged. "I didn't catch a good look at him. I've been busy studying this ficus tree." He jabbed Cindi's tea mug at the drooping leaves of the plant in the corner. Some of the tea sloshed over onto Mr. Paigely's foot, but, now into a debate about Earl Gray versus English Breakfast tea with Cindi, he didn't notice it. "That ficus needs more light," Pantelli declared.

"Er ... yes. I'll tell the manager," I promised. "Now, Pantelli. You've got to study *Jon*. I want to establish for sure that he's Leo. Hey! I have an idea."

"Please, Di. Remember, I'm in a weakened condition."

"This'd be easy if you were in a *dead* condition." I grabbed Jon's cell phone, which he'd left on the desk. I also grabbed a pen and scribbled on the blotter. "Here's the number to this phone. Jon's going to bring everyone back here to pick you up, once you've regained your strength. I heard him say so to Mr. Paigely. When he does, you'll either recognize him as the guy in the window or you won't. Phone me right away and let me know."

I indicated the office desk phone that he could use to call me. Pantelli regarded its numerous buttons, for different locals around the theater, with some doubt. "Uh, why don't you just wait here with me?"

"I can't." I waved to Frank, who'd appeared in the doorway. "Frank and I have to get ready to rehearse a scene together."

With a friendly punch to Pantelli's shoulder, I stuffed the cell phone in my jacket pocket and hurried out with Frank. The last glimpse I had of Pantelli, he was continuing to stare in bewilderment at the phone, as if it were some odd tree specimen he'd never seen before ...

16.
Positive identification

In the dressing room I shared with Cindi, I simply pulled on my costume over my jeans and sweatshirt. It didn't matter, because the costume for that nighttime scene was a bulky, billowy nightgown. Cut corners, I like to say.

Frank's costume was more complicated — a tux and some weird stiff white shirt that took ages to fasten up — so I waited around in the hallway for him. Overhead, the footsteps of my class thundered as Jon showed them round the stage, explaining stuff like what "wings" were and how the lights and curtains worked. To my surprise, I felt kind of proud, as if Jon were showing the kids around my own home.

It was a less pleasant surprise when I heard footsteps on the stairs, as well as a fat, silky voice I recognized to be Mr. Murdock's.

"I am very sincere about promoting the arts. But I'm also counting on this production of Wilkie Collins' classic novel to promote my line of jewelry. We'll be selling moonstone rings in the lobby during intermission and after the show."

"Your line of jewelry ... right. Er, Mr. Murdock, tell me about this kid who I understand is a singing sensation."

I guessed the second speaker to be a reporter. When the two of them descended the last of the stairs, I saw I was right. He was a pale, rumpled young man jotting notes down rapidly on a steno-pad.

"Yes, a loud girl," said Mr. Murdock, rather disapprovingly. He paused for some heavy wheezes, catching his breath. He then poked a puffy forefinger against the reporter's notepad. "One thing you ought to mention in your write-up is this fantasmo wardrobe designer we got. Lemme tell ya, her costumes are exquisite. Real delicate-like, real — "

It was then that they spotted me loitering outside Frank's dressing room, in the crookedly-pulled-on nightgown over bulky jeans and sweatshirt, with muddy hiking shoes jutting out beneath.

" ... delicate-like, as I said," Mr. Murdock finished weakly.

"Oh, hi," I said, trying to make the best of the situation. "I'm — uh, I'm just heading into a conference with Jon. You know, about character development 'n' stuff."

Anything to escape Mr. Murdock. Stepping back, I pushed at the door of Jon's office and fled inside, even as the producer feebly objected, "But Jon's upstairs ... "

The plaid jacket. While I was here I might as well get it and show Frank.

As I was pulling the jacket off its hanger, I heard Frank's amused voice, "Come out, come out, wherever you are!"

I peered round Jon's office door. Frank popped his handsome face round to greet me, making me jump. The formal Victorian-era tuxedo made him look more charming than ever. He laughed. "The evil ogre, Uncle Nigel, has departed, my sweet. He waddled back upstairs with much huffing and puffing."

Evil ogre seemed a disrespectful way to refer to his uncle, not to mention the person, however disagreeable, who was giving a lot of us an important break in show business. However, at the cheery twinkle in Frank's eyes I couldn't help giggling. "I was hiding because Mr. Murdock said I was loud. As in, *too* loud."

"I love your loudness," Frank told me solemnly. "It'll send thrills up the audience's spine. Garland had that. Streisand has it. Now, Ms. Dinah Galloway has it as well."

I glowed at his praise. "Aw, *well* ..."

"Plus, you're the only living soul who can sing louder than Cindi can scream. Unless you count an elephant's trumpeting."

"Uh-huh," I said more doubtfully. Somehow his second comment wasn't quite so flattering.

"Just keep it up, kid. You're doing magnif — "

He paused, staring at the jacket I'd stuffed under my arm. "Hey, what's this? Don't tell me faded, moth-eaten plaid is the latest clothing trend at Lord Bithersby."

He was looking so horrified that I giggled again. Frank himself was always mega chic. He wore the same kind of loose, casual, never-wrinkly stuff that the young men in Madge's fashion magazines did.

Before I could reply, there were more footsteps on the stairs, this time thundering ones. My classmates were descending for a tour of this level.

With Jon as their guide.

I clutched the jacket. I couldn't let Jon see me with it — he'd realize I was onto him! "Frank," I whispered, "we gotta get out of here."

His face regained its usual good humor. Somehow I had to make him understand the urgency. "Fast!" I pleaded.

With my free hand I grabbed at the knob of the door to the only escape route available: the staircase into the forbidden basement.

Masses of wires, strung like cobwebs. A great gray clanking furnace. A ghostly white water heater.

Then there were the dark, musty depths behind these, leading who knew where. Above, suspended from the ceiling, swayed a bare lightbulb; Frank's head had knocked against it. As the bulb swung, real cobwebs gleamed at us out of the dark, musty depths. No one had ventured there in years.

"You sure know how to show a guy a good time," remarked Frank. "Y'know, kid, if you'd wanted to talk, we *could* have just gone to a coffee shop."

I laughed. Frank could always make me feel better. "It's about this padded jacket. It's the costume the mysterious Leo wore when he tried to give me a scare in the Windmill Café." I fished the gray wig out of a jacket arm and waggled it in front of him. "See what I mean?"

"No." Frank approached me, his handsome forehead creased with puzzlement. "I don't see.

Besides, I thought we had a deal. If you were planning any more investigating, you were going to tell me about it first."

"Oh, this costume was an accidental discovery," I informed him airily. "I caught my sleeve on Jon's closet door handle and — well, never mind for now. What I wanted to say is that this proves Jon is — "

Brrring! Brrring! I'd forgotten I was carrying the cell phone. I rummaged in my pocket for it, impatient at being disturbed.

It was Pantelli. "Hey, Di, sorry I took so long. I couldn't figure out these dumb telephone lines. I pushed one button and went straight through to someplace called Acropolis Pizza. When I asked for you, this lady who answered said, 'Diner? This ain't a diner, it's a pizzeria.' Then I had to find somebody who knew how to access a free line."

He took a deep breath. "Anyhow, that guy *is* the same guy I saw through the window."

I'd been right, then. Jon was Leo.

"So it's Jon. Um, great," I said. And it should have been great. My powers of deduction had triumphed.

But all I felt was a kind of sinking disappointment. Definitely more *um* than *great*. If only Mother didn't like Jon so much ... if only *I* didn't like him so much. Grimacing, I gave Frank what was probably the limpest thumbs-up in history.

In my glumness I didn't immediately realize that Pantelli was stammering out a reply.

"Jon? Uh ... isn't he the director dude?"

"Yeah." I heaved a big sigh. "In a way I wish you hadn't recognized him." I shrugged apologetically at Frank, who by now was frowning down at me. I couldn't blame him. Who'd want to be stuck in this dungeon-like place with me? At this moment I didn't like being stuck with me either.

"But I didn't recognize *him*," said Pantelli.

"*What?*"

"I didn't recognize the director dude. He's not your mysterious Leo."

I clutched my hair. Though if I pulled it out in here, the falling strands would probably constitute a fire hazard. "Pantelli, has your brain caught one of those tree diseases you're always talking about? *What are you saying?*"

His next words cut through me like a shard of ice.

"The guy you went off with is the one I recognized. *He's* Leo."

17.
Uh-oh, to put it mildly

Meanwhile, Frank was standing right over me. Looming. Why had I never noticed before that his oh-so-charming smile was never reflected in his eyes? Sure, his eyes sparkled, but so does snow.

"You don't want to be carrying those around," he murmured, taking the padded plaid jacket and gray wig from me. "They ought to be burned."

He tossed them far back into the basement's cobwebby depths. It occurred to me that he was probably wishing he could do the same to me. How stupid I'd been to trust him. He'd said I could tell *him* my suspicions, but I shouldn't confide in Jon for fear I'd be tossed out of the show. *I was a kid once, too,* he'd said. *I remember how important it was to tell the grown-ups everything.*

To think I'd suspected his uncle of being Leo. Now it made sense that Mr. Murdock had told Jon he wanted me ousted from the show. *Frank had asked him to.* No wonder Frank had been so disgusted at Jon for not obeying Mr. Murdock! Then Frank had quickly recovered and pretended to be on my side.

Oh, he was good. The night of the sushi dinner, Frank had even pretended he wanted to confront Jon! He'd known all along I wouldn't let him, because I didn't want to cause trouble or be booted out of the show.

And the incident at the Windmill Café. After shoving me into the washroom, he must've hastened back to the theater just in time to meet Cindi and Graham the Piano Man for lunch at Dairy Queen. Of course! *Cindi and Graham had left for lunch late.*

Frank was more than good. He was slick.

And me?

"A total sap," I groaned.

"About what, Dinah?" asked Frank, his green eyes bright.

"This is sap season, all right," Pantelli said in my ear. "My favorite time of year: maple syrup. *Num.*"

I jumped. Pantelli! "You're still there," I said, stupid with relief.

The cell phone was sliding from my hand —

my palm was that clammy. Wiping it off on the nightgown, I gripped the phone again. "Um, Pantelli," I said, managing a ghastly smile at Frank, "we'll be right up. Frank and I snuck into the basement. To talk. Us theat-ah types, dontcha know." I let out a high, silly laugh.

"Uh, Dinah," Pantelli said doubtfully, "is the air maybe a bit *thin* down where you are?"

I was so jittery by now that I released a whole series of silly laughs with no trouble at all. My objective: fool Frank into thinking I was too much of an idiot for him to worry about, or him to stuff into the dark recesses of the basement along with the plaid jacket and wig. Maybe permanently.

Which I was sure he would like to do, from the calculating way he was studying me.

Okay, so act idiotic, Dinah. It's not difficult for you most of the time.

Gulp.

Yeah, but *having* to do something is way different.

Why oh why hadn't I paid more attention to Jon's acting advice?

Hey. You did pay *some* attention, Dinah. Focus. Become Coretta Cuff in such a situation. She'd be resourceful. She'd fool a villain.

Then, suddenly, I *was* Coretta. I was a kid stuck

among a bunch of flirtatious, high society guys and gals. I knew exactly what she'd say.

"Oh, Frank," I gushed, turning my ghastly smile into an adoring one. "I didn't even want those smelly old clothes. I just wanted — well, *you* know. I admit I'm only eleven, but I'm not without feelings. Couldn't we have a meaningful talk about our future?"

"I'm going to be sick," Pantelli announced in my ear.

I overheard Mr. Paigely fret, near Pantelli, "You're going to be sick again? But you're not on the bus now."

Meanwhile, a smug, satisfied expression had settled over Frank's handsome — make that *too* handsome — features. "You're a cute kid," he smirked. "A little goofy, but cute."

With that he gave a mocking bow and gestured towards the stairs. Hoisting the voluminous folds of nightgown, I thundered up the basement steps. Phew!

But —

Careful, girl, warned a cautious little voice inside me. You'll have to be on your guard. Those cold green eyes of his will be watching you now, all the time ...

I shuddered.

"Very good, Dinah," Jon praised as clapping, foot-stomping and whistles broke out from my classmates, Mr. Paigely and the other cast members.

Frank and I had just performed our song, an original one written for this production, "Can I Believe in You?" Of course, I now knew that I couldn't, not in him.

Jon continued, "You've caught Coretta Cuff's uneasiness about the fiancé perfectly. Good acting!"

Um, not really. In the script, Coretta came round to trusting the fiancé later on. This was one case where art was *not* imitating life.

At our local park, someone had swept all the leaves into huge piles. It was an annual tradition for us to rollerblade rapidly between the piles, using them for an obstacle course.

"Yooo-hoo, Dinah!" called Mrs. Dubuque from the sidewalk.

Startled, I almost bladed into a pile of leaves. "Hi, Mrs. Dubuque." I put on my phony, bared-teeth smile. Somehow when either of the Dubuques wanted to talk to me, it was never good news.

Mrs. Dubuque squinted through the tennis court's chain-link fence at me. "How's Wilfred?"

Wilfred? Mrs. Dubuque was inquiring about my *cat*? The Dubuques were well-known animal loathers.

"Probably sleeping," I said.

"Because I heard him give a painful-sounding meow on Halloween night," Mrs. Dubuque explained, her pudgy features scrunched in bewilderment. "It was such an *odd* noise ... "

My wolf imitation! Boy, couldn't anyone get it straight? However, I shrugged and looked as cheerful and innocent as possible.

Mrs. Dubuque continued, in a rather peevish tone, "My goodness, the noise was so loud, so piercing, we couldn't think of anything else till it stopped." She ambled off.

"Some wolf you were!" Pantelli then jeered as we resumed zooming between the piles. "Hey, Di!" He caught up to me. "You don't — you were just kidding about liking that Frank dude, right?"

I turned and shoved him backward into a leaf pile. This, too, was part of the annual tradition. "I'd prefer listening to you talk about trees for a year than spend a minute with Frank!"

I bladed away, leaving Pantelli looking ridiculously pleased. I guess not too many people encouraged him in his tree monologues.

I wasn't feeling at all pleased. I'd told Jon the whole story about Frank — "But you thought *I* was a would-be thief before," he'd reminded me.

Memo to self: Never admit to a non-suspect

that you previously considered him to be one.

Jon had grinned, and I knew he thought I was imagining the whole thing.

"It was the song 'Ain't That A Kick in the Head,' I explained. "Leo kept saying, 'Ain't that a kick in the head' — and then I happened to overhear you telling Mother you liked that song."

Uh-oh. I hoped Jon wouldn't ask me where I'd overheard that.

He didn't. He just grinned again. "I often give Frank a lift home after rehearsal. That song is on one of the CDs I play in my car. Small wonder he's got the words stuck in his mind."

Jon ruffled my hair. "I'll warn Mr. Murdock about some, er, rumors of a possible heist," he promised.

Then his expression turned anxious. "Uh — it might be better if you don't share your theories with our producer. Cross as he is with most people, Mr. M. actually does seem to *like* his nephew."

Now, blading past Pantelli, I sighed aloud, "Everybody likes Frank. That's the problem."

I waved at Pantelli, who'd struggled up and was brushing leaves off himself, and skimmed round the tennis courts some more.

I pictured the moonstone ring again, and how, like the moon, it shifted into different shapes and shadows, like the expressions on a face. In my imagination the face became Frank's, smiling charmingly at me and mocking me for not being able to figure out his plans.

I put the image of the man in the moonstone out of my mind and thought instead about Mrs. Dubuque. About how she'd blamed Wilfred for my wolf yowl. It was so dumb, when Wilfred was way too cowardly most of the time even to venture outsi—

I glided to a stop. In all her prattling, Mrs. Dubuque had said something significant. Something that loitered now at the edges of my mind, just out of reach.

What was it? She'd talked about Wilfred ... about yowling ... If only I could remember.

Pantelli bladed up and, taking advantage of my stillness, shoved me into a pile of leaves.

18.
Angela again

When you need advice about what to do, go to the top, I always say.

"Dear God, I'm stuck."

I was praying at our church, St. Cecilia's, that Saturday afternoon. Mother had brought Jon, Madge and me there for a concert by some visiting choir. I thought I'd get my requests in to the Big Guy before the choir started.

I paused to peek out from under my eyelids. The choir was filing up to the front. I just had time to finish.

"See, everybody thinks Beak-Nose is in New York. But she can't be. She and Frank are planning to steal the moonstone.

"What's worse, nobody believes me about any of this. If I could just have some *help*, God, in focusing on the problem, like Jon and Mr. Paigely are always telling me to do in math."

Crossing myself, I got up from kneeling and sat back on the bench with Mother and Madge. Then it occurred to me I should tack on a P.S. I clenched my eyes shut again. "I don't expect very much," I assured God.

This time I'd spoken louder than I thought. A fat man in the pew ahead of me turned and scowled. "What do you mean, you don't expect much? Young lady, the Junior Girls' Choir is one of the finest in the land. How *dare* you."

The sourpuss. When he'd turned towards the front again, I curled my fingers into a pretend claw and lowered them almost to the top of his heavily oiled hair. This struck both me and Pantelli, sitting a little farther along in the same pew, as most amusing — not, however, our mothers. They both made furious signals for me to stop.

"GLORIA!"

This first word from the visiting choir rang out into the silence, startling us. Well, at least those of us who hadn't been paying attention. "Whoever this Gloria is, she better get up there quickly," I joked to Madge.

"Sssshhh!"

The choir let loose another flurry of Glorias. I

sighed. It was going to be a long stretch to the post-concert reception, my favorite part of these things.

Downstairs, in the church hall, there'd be platters of dainty fluffy sandwiches, the crusts cut off and the centres creamy with egg or tuna salad, or ham and cheese. I loved these sandwiches. Due to their tiny size you could cram a couple into your mouth at a time — very efficient — even while you were reaching for more. And those radishes that Mother and her friends sliced into flower shapes. Num.

My stomach grumbled, earning me sharp glances from Mother and Madge. "C'mon," I objected. "It's not my fault that I'm starv — "

Sudden silvery notes, like a clear, pure mountain stream, poured out.

"Gloria in Excelsis Deo!" sang a soloist.

I forgot Frank, dainty sandwiches, the disapproval of Mother and Madge. All I could think about was the music this soloist was making. I've said before that her notes sounded like silver, but they were more beautiful than any metal. They were — how can I put it? They were like the way your heart feels when it's totally happy.

I stretched and fidgeted to be able to see around Sourpuss to the soloist, but I already knew who she was. Only one person sang like that.

"Like the angels," wept my mother, mopping her eyes with a hanky.

"Not angels. Angela," I corrected her, and there was real pride in my voice. Though I'd only met Angela Bridey once and hadn't even liked her, I felt proud of her for singing like that.

Angela finished. There was the same stunned silence that had resulted when she'd tried out for the Coretta Cuff part. Like my mother, a lot of women, and even some men, were sniffling. Mrs. Audia, whose shoulders were actually heaving with the force of her sobs, passed a tissue box down the pew.

"Wow," I breathed. I realized I was grinning idiotically out of sheer pleasure and admiration. This time I didn't feel any rivalry at all. "Talk about your godsends," I told Mother. "Angela's one, for sure."

I had to shout this, because the applause had started. Jon, on the other side of Madge and Mother, shouted back at me, "You're both great singers, Dinah. The difference is that Angela does sing like the angels. You sing for the rest of us who are trying to get up there. You express all our yearnings."

"You would have liked my dad," I informed Jon

after the concert, as everybody stood downstairs in the church hall, balancing plates of dainty sandwiches and glasses of punch. My plate was piled particularly high, half with egg sandwiches, half with brownies. I'd plunked radishes all over this sculpture. A lot of people were glancing at my mountainous plate: in awe, I supposed.

"You see," I continued to Jon, who for some reason was fighting off a smile, "Dad said stuff like that to me. You know, about expressing what's in your heart when you sing. Or when you do any kind of creative thing." With a pinwheel-shaped egg sandwich, I gestured to my sister. "Like Madge with her drawing." I tucked the sandwich, plus a radish, in and beamed.

Madge was too busy staring at my plate — envious, I guessed — to reply. In any case, I then felt a timid tapping on my shoulder.

"Hi," said Angela Bridey.

"Hmm," I said through a fresh mouthful of egg salad.

Angela smiled shyly. When she did this, she lost the pale, pinched look that reminded me so much of her aunt. In fact, smiling, she didn't resemble her aunt at all.

"My aunt was — um, in a hurry to get us out of the Livingston Theater the night of the auditions,"

Angela said, blushing with the effort of speaking to me. "I've always wanted to tell you how wonderful you were. I mean, so — " She hesitated.

"Loud?" I supplied.

"We-ell, more than that. So, um ... so warm. Oh, I can't say it properly, but ... " She blushed deeper.

I exclaimed, "As a matter of fact, I think *you're* great. Really incredible." I crunched a radish, trying to think of how to compliment her adequately. My gaze fell to my plate. I'd been so looking forward to stuffing back every morsel ...

"Here," I declared. On a rare selfless impulse, I handed the plate to her. "This is for you."

"Th-thanks," said Angela — and just as I was hoping she'd say she had an allergy to egg salad and have to return the plate, Pantelli interrupted.

"What is this, a mutual admiration society? C'mon, Di, they've set out my mom's dark-chocolate-fudge brownies."

Angela and I traded goggly-eyed glances. That was all it took. Along with Pantelli, we raced to the dessert table. I mean, discussing the art of singing was all right. But we had our priorities.

Thoughtfully, I licked dark-chocolate-fudge frosting off my thumb. I wanted to raise the subject of

Beak-Nose with Angela, yet not offend her. After all, the woman was Angela's aunt. I couldn't just blurt out my suspicions about Beak-Nose planning a heist.

Subtlety was required, I decided. Extreme subtlety.

I polished off the frosting from another thumb and asked, "So, Angela, are you aware of any criminal tendencies in your aunt?"

Uh-oh. Maybe that hadn't sounded quite as subtle as I'd hoped. Angela regarded me in astonishment — then giggled.

"Aunt Violet is kind of ... forbidding, you might say. Actually she and my parents aren't speaking right now." She grimaced. "My parents are mad at her for dragging me out that night to the *Moonstone* auditions. I was at her place for dinner, and she took me along without asking them first. I didn't want to go, you see. I like performing classical music, not belting out show tunes. No offence," Angela added quickly. "Aunt Vi was determined to get us 'in,' as she kept saying. She was angry when I didn't win the part — even a couple of days later she was ranting that she couldn't believe it."

So she put Frank up to phoning me at school, I thought. To try and scare me out of accepting the part.

"She's Dad's older sister," Angela was saying, "but they don't have much in common: Dad's easy-going, and Aunt Vi's tough and ambitious. Not exactly a walking laugh fest, if you know what I mean.

"Anyhow, after that night Mom told Aunt Vi we didn't need her help with my singing, thank you very much! They had a huge row, and Aunt Vi stomped off. She threw back over her shoulder, like a sharp stone, the comment that she was heading to New York to find work. And that she didn't care if she ever saw us again."

I shook my head, wishing I could clear the confusion out of it. "That's where Jon said she was going, too. But it doesn't make sense."

Because I was sure Beak-Nose and Frank were planning to steal the moonstone, but I was too polite to add that.

"Oh, she might find work there," Angela shrugged. "Aunt Vi's a very convincing actress. She could play any part."

Several people, including Sourpuss, came up to Angela to congratulate her on her performance. I edged off to one side and thought hard.

Was there some way Beak-Nose could help steal the moonstone long-distance?

A ceiling light danced on Sourpuss's oily hair,

distracting me. He gestured a lot, and each time he did, the pool of light slid from one part of his head to another. It was useless. I couldn't think.

" ... so marvelous that you were with the Royal Opera!" Sourpuss was enthusing, as Angela, by now thoroughly embarrassed, shot desperate glances back and forth, seeking a means of escape. She'd stay, though; she was the polite type. Such a disadvantage in life, I reflected.

"Imagine!" Sourpuss exclaimed. "The R.O.!"

"R.O.?" interrupted Pantelli, who, like me, was free of politeness.

Everyone stared at him. He grinned back. "B.O. is more like it." With a sculpted radish he waved at our classmate, Lee Ann Hornblower, who'd just come into the hall.

Not knowing Lee Ann, none of the other people within hearing range remotely understood what he was talking about. I forced a phony laugh. "This is my friend Pantelli," I explained, steering him away from them. "He's always been a bit ... different."

"It was a great concert," Jon told Mother. "Just the break I needed before the play opens. The food was great too." He glanced at Pantelli and me. "Well, what there was of it."

"That's not fair," I objected. "There was a whole

table we didn't even get to."

Jon and Mother laughed. There was a kind of shy silence, and Jon offered his hand to her. "Thanks again. I know you've got your car here, so I won't offer you a lift home."

They shook hands and then just held them. "Well," said Jon at last, "I guess I'll be off — "

"No!" Madge blurted out.

We all gaped at her. She managed a weak smile. "I mean ... " She gulped. "I mean, I think you should offer Mother a lift, Jon. And stay out with her a while. For dinner, if you want."

Madge frowned, and I saw that her eyes had tears in them. Dad, I thought suddenly. She's letting go of Dad.

For a second there was a lump in my own throat. I cleared it and instructed Jon sternly: "On a first date you should bring her home by ten *at the latest*." I'd got this out of one of Madge's teen magazines. Not that I, Dinah Galloway, aged eleven, would ever really *read* stuff like that. Browse once in a while, maybe.

Mother was tomato red. "Dinah, Madge, I'm sure Jon has plans — "

"I'll toss the plans out," Jon assured her. He lifted her hand. "Anyhow, since we're evidently glued together, we'd better take your daughters up on their offer. I'd sure like to," he added — and from the way they smiled at each other, I could tell their gazes were fast getting glued together too.

Mother did succeed in peeling her eyes away for one last, motherly glance. "Till ten," she told us. And followed up with that most *un*motherly thing.

A giggle.

19.
The secret of the scream

The bandleader winked at me. From between the curtains I grinned and winked back. The band was breezing through all the songs that would be featured once the curtain went up. I snapped my fingers, swayed to the music and wished I could go out now, without waiting, to sing.

"So I take it opening night jitters aren't a big problem for you," Jon observed.

I shook my head. I loved it all. The panic and excitement. The thudding footsteps and frantic murmurs of the cast and crew rushing around. Even the retching behind me — Cindi, throwing up from nervousness.

I loved the too-sweet smell of the heavy make-up the cast had to wear, competing with the perfumes and colognes wafting up from the audience, that was milling into their seats behind the band.

Jon peered through the curtains with me. "There's your mother and Madge."

"Madge's boyfriend is supposed to be joining them. His plane's running a bit late," I told Jon.

I recalled with satisfaction the rather curt call Jack had placed to our house the night before. He'd told Madge he was coming back to find out just what this Frank business was all about.

"Wonder what he meant by 'frank business'?" she'd puzzled to Mother and me afterward. "He and I have always been frank and open with each other. What's his problem?"

I chuckled to myself. *I'd* got Jack to return. Was I wily, or what?

Not that Frank himself was anything to be amused about. He was going to swipe the Murdock moonstone, I was sure of it, and I still couldn't figure out how. I hadn't yet been very wily about that.

I scanned the audience. The person I was looking for wasn't a friend or loved one. It was Violet Bridey. Her leaving the city just didn't make sense to me. Beak-Nose *had* to be around. Otherwise, Frank would be on his own, and who ever heard of a jewel thief gang of one?

"AAACH!" Cindi was on a fresh bout of retching into the empty carton.

At least she'd assumed it was empty. A shrill, aggrieved voice demanded, "Hey! Whaddya think you're doing to my make-up case?"

"Case?" Cindi repeated weakly.

The other woman, the actress who played the maid, declared, "Sure! I pack all my cosmetics in a cardboard box. And now they're covered in — "

She let loose a horrified scream.

"Not a bad scream," I remarked to Jon. Giving up on trying to spot Beak-Nose, I let the curtains fall together again. "But no one can rival Cindi."

Except me, possibly. While waiting to go onstage in the first act, I grinned at something Frank had kept teasing me about. He'd said that with my belting-out voice, I and only I could match Cindi for volume.

Oops. What was I doing? I shouldn't be enjoying the humor of a villain. I immediately scowled — causing Jon, who was beside me, to look anxious. After all, a funny moment was supposed to be occurring onstage.

At her vanity, Miss Verinder (Cindi), fluffing powder all over her face, was fluffing the air around her, too. As a result, her maid (the actress with the ruined makeup case) was having an attack of coughing.

The audience laughed, and Jon relaxed. He was

concerned that no funny moments fall flat. That was deadly to a play, he maintained.

Just as I was wondering whether Frank had been right to say I could out-sing Cindi's screams, Jon gave me a nudge.

"Kid, I think you may be suffering from reverse stage fright. Too *little* nervousness! It's almost your cue, Dinah."

What! I was supposed to go on now? I gulped, and the hundreds of butterflies that must've been hiding in my stomach up till now rose gleefully and fluttered.

"Um, Jon, how badly do you want Coretta onstage at this time? In my opinion, she kind of detracts from the scene."

"She *is* the scene, Dinah."

Now it was my cue: the maid had finished coughing. Jon gave me a shove — not a very dignified way to launch a show business career, but there you have it. Just in time I remembered to slip my glasses off and tuck them into a pocket of my frilly dress.

Yech, a dress. What was worse, there were layers and layers of crinolines underneath. The audience promptly got a full view of these, because I had to make my entrance in a series of cartwheels.

It was all part of me, being the one kid in the

show, adding a bit of liveliness to an otherwise fairly formal Victorian setting.

Jon had brought in a gymnastics teacher to show me not just how to get my cartwheels right, but how to get them *wrong*, too.

Here's why: just as Jon had directed me to, I botched the final cartwheel and crashed my feet sideways, right at the maid's ample rear end.

Being clumsy on purpose is harder than you might think. This had taken hours of rehearsal. The maid shrieked, the audience laughed — and then all the hours were worth it.

I got into my part, and that scene and the next one flew by. I liked Coretta. We were so similar! She was a detective — and she had tons of energy.

Boy, this was fun! You did the same things you did at rehearsal, but it was different. On most days, the area beyond the rim of the stage was just a bunch of canvas-covered metal seats. With the lights up, this area darkened and expanded like the night sky, going on forever. You felt like the whole universe was holding its breath, watching *you*.

I exited the stage, and then the play was back to a more serious tone. The black-leotarded dancers glided out for their mysterious shadow dance. As the jewel thieves, they were shadowing the Verinder mansion, waiting to slip in and grab the moonstone.

Beak-Nose was like a shadow too, I thought. She'd disappeared — yet I knew she was waiting to slip in and grab the Murdock moonstone, along with Frank. Where *was* she?

I scanned the audience again, a kind of point-less exercise because against the lights I could only see the front row, and vaguely. There were Mother, Madge and Pantelli.

"Hee hee hee!"

A skinny elbow prodded me aside. It was the little cleaning woman, clothed in musty navy velvet — her Sunday best, I guessed — with a worn brown hat clapped somewhat askew atop her wispy head. Her few teeth were bared in a delighted grin.

"Ain't that somethin'! Jest lookit all o' them shadows prancin' around!"

But of course the shadow I wanted to "lookit" wasn't there.

The appearance of the Murdock moonstone drew lots of applause. From the wings I could see peo-ple in the front row, even more or less sensible ones like Mother and Madge, straining forward, their mouths round with wonder. "Ooooo," went everyone.

As Miss Verinder, Cindi had to flounce around the stage, which at the moment was her bedroom, fluttering her moonstone-ringed hand. Mr. Murdock had insisted this scene be written in as a way of promoting the souvenir moonstone rings that his sales reps were hawking in the lobby.

The neat part came at the end of the scene. The silhouettes of the jewel thieves appeared against the windows, causing more *oooo's*, but this time of surprise. What I couldn't understand was Miss Verinder (Cindi) not seeing the silhouettes, since there were so many of them. I'd asked Jon about this. He'd explained that people in plays were often unaware of things the audience knew. Dramatic irony, he'd called it, and had begun to cite examples from Shakespeare and other works. At which I'd edged away from him.

When Cindi came back into the wings, even I broke down and *oooo'd* over the ring. "It *is* like the moon," I exclaimed as she turned her hand this way and that. "You can see all these changing shapes, even a face."

One of Mr. Murdock's security guards, looming grimly beside us like a pillar, scowled into the ring. "Nope," he said at last. "I don't see nuthin', except a huge price tag, maybe." And his broad, square shoulders quaked at his joke.

The ring darkened. Another shadow was bending over it. Frank was smiling into it as if it were a bowl of soup he was about to lap up.

Which, in a way, he was. Why couldn't I figure out how?

"Now you're the man in the moonstone," Cindi teased him. She stretched her finger at an angle so that the stone reflected the pink of his skin. Well, of his stage makeup, anyway.

Frank laughed fondly, but I, beyond pretending, just gave him a cold stare. He grinned. "Alas, our Di has become a temperamental star already," and gave my chin a friendly pinch.

Ouch! A hard pinch, not so friendly after all. A warning?

Then it was time for the "Blue Moon" number. My agent, Mr. Wellman, had told me this was a vital moment in my stage career. It was my first chance at belting out a song — and if I blew it, possibly my last.

Talk about putting the pressure on.

"You'll be fine, Dinah," Mr. Wellman had laughed, visiting me in the dressing room before the show. "Like an old song says, 'Dinah, is there anything finah?' "

He'd turned to Cindi to offer her a pep talk as well, but she'd forestalled him with a faint scream of protest. "Puh-leeze, Mr. W. I heard what you said to

Di. Your kind of encouragement I can do without."

"I know you'll both make me proud," Mrs. Wellman had assured us. With another merry laugh, he'd exited ...

Onstage, waiting for Cindi to finish her part of the song, I felt the butterflies return in full force. I took deep breaths, the cure everyone advised for nervousness.

As long as Cindi was singing, I was on a darkened spot of the stage — so was Frank, to my right. Being in the dark meant I could see into the audience.

I could see into the audience ... uh-oh. In the nick of time I remembered to snatch my glasses off. Phew! Cindi was just finishing. The spotlight was about to shine on me.

There. That silvery blue light, as if poured from a pail. I was in the middle of it, like a girl on the moon, with blackness all around me. I had to be lonely as the moon, too, in my role as Coretta Cuff, far from her dad.

Blue moon, you saw me standing alone ...

I was singing the first part softly, as Jon had directed me to. My voice had a catch in it — for Coretta's sadness, and for mine.

"Then let your voice go. Pitch it to the moon," Jon had instructed.

you saw me standing alo-o-one ...

Boy, if Mrs. Dubuque thought my Halloween yowl was loud, she oughtta hear me now.

without a dream in my heart ...

Mrs. Dubuque had said, *The noise was so piercing we couldn't think of anything else.* Those were the words of Mrs. Dubuque that I'd been trying to recall ... *so piercing we couldn't think of anything else.*

Suddenly I knew why Mrs. Dubuque's words had bothered me. They'd reminded me of what Frank always egged me on to do. *You could probably out-sing one of Cindi's screams*, he'd teased. *You could do it. Nobody would even think of her.*

At least, I'd thought he was teasing. I'd taken it as a kind of fun dare. Like that evening in the lobby, when I'd out-volumed Cindi.

But maybe he hadn't egged me on for fun.

I started in on my last, knock-'em-dead line: *WITHOUT A LOVE OF MY ...*

Deep breath. I was to hold the note of the final word, *OWN*, for a long time that would shiver the audience's spines with excitement and awe, ensuring the future of my singing career.

I started in on the final note:

O-O-O-O —

Then I got it. What Frank had intended.

He'd wanted me to sing so loudly that nobody would notice anything else.

I never got to the *n* in *own*. I stopped singing, right then.

Beside me, in the dark, Cindi was screaming.

20.
That nose looks awfully familiar ...

Jamming on my glasses, I rushed out of the spotlight to her. "Cindi, stop screaming. Tell me what happened."

Her scream fizzled out, like the whistle of a kettle that's been unplugged. She began gulping with sobs. "H-he k-k-kissed me!"

The audience, left staring at an empty patch of silver spotlight, gave a few uncertain laughs. Had the scene, supposedly about three people feeling sad, taken an abrupt comedic turn?

"The-then he stole th-the ring. Th-the Murdock moonstone!"

"WHAT!"

A plump silhouette bounced up from the center of the front row. It stomped, wheezing, up the steps to the stage.

"MY RING!" shouted Mr. Murdock — and as

the audience, thinking this was a funky new plot twist, started clapping, he snapped, "BE QUIET, YOU IDIOTS! Will someone put on the *lights?*"

They flooded on immediately, from all directions. "YEOW!" shouted Mr. Murdock, kneading his eyelids with chubby white fingers. "I just want my ring! WHERE IS IT?"

In response, security guards clomped onstage and glowered.

Meanwhile, I'd been peering at the audience, whose astonished faces, above their jewels and cravats, were also now exposed in the blazing lights. Specifically, I'd focused on my agent, Mr. Wellman. It hadn't been hard to pick him out. He was the only audience member with his face buried, weeping, in his hands.

So much for my career launch, I thought sinkingly.

It was then I realized the security guards were glowering at Cindi and me. Mr. Murdock waddled towards us, a fleshy forefinger jabbing the air. "WHERE ... IS ... IT?"

Choking with tears, Cindi raised a trembling hand, the one that, in earlier scenes, had borne the creamy, mysterious moonstone ring. Her now bare fingers gestured into the wings, at Frank.

"Me!" protested Frank, laughing. He shrugged, ever-handsome, ever-charming. "Darlin', when you screamed, I rushed over to you. Now, it was dark, so I couldn't swear as to what happened next, but you did raise your hand and — I thought — throw something."

He frowned, charmingly of course, and considered. "Yes, you threw something ... into the audience, if I had to guess."

"WHAT!" Mr. Murdock swung his still outstretched, chubby forefinger like a wrecking ball until it faced the audience. "NO ONE LEAVES!" he spluttered. "YOU'RE TO BE SEARCHED, EACH ONE OF YOU!"

Uproar. Objections and insults surged from the audience, tidal-wave style. People got up and began shoving at each other to get out into the aisle. To get out, period. Crumpled theater programs rained on Mr. Murdock, bouncing off the pink bald spot at the top of his head.

Meanwhile, at a bellowed command from Mr. Murdock, two security guards advanced on Cindi. They clamped burly hands on her shoulders. "Oh no you don't," I yelled — and delivered fierce kicks to their shins.

"Ow!" — that was me, not them. Their legs were like stone.

"Don't panic, Cindi," Jon said, hurrying up to us. "Murdock won't get away with this. I'll get you a lawyer, if necessary. The thing to remember is, stay calm. Okay? *Calm.*"

"Okay," quavered Cindi — and promptly fractured our eardrums with her loudest scream ever.

The cast and crew, stuffed into the wings to watch, called encouraging words to her. A couple of the actors tore pages out of their scripts. Scrunching these up, they hurled them at Mr. Murdock, increasing the storm of paper already attacking him from the audience. The producer had never been very popular.

The only person not in an uproar was Frank. He lounged at the side of the stage, relaxed and amused.

Then, for an instant, his eyes met mine. They were cool and clear, tranquil as two green ponds would be on a day unruffled by breeze.

He knew exactly what was going on.

He was — I almost choked on the realization — *controlling* what was going on.

Without even thinking about it, I opened my mouth and let out the belting-out-est middle C of my life.

Well, that silenced everyone. Stopped 'em dead in

their tracks. The audience members who'd been cramming out the doors paused to turn and stare. The security guards' fingers froze on Cindi's shoulders. She was able to wriggle free and step away. Mr. Murdock quit yelling and spluttering.

In the audience, Mr. Wellman, who'd been looking greenish and ready to faint, recovered some of his color and regarded me rather admiringly.

The only problem with being a showstopper is that you have to follow it up with something. "It was Frank who grabbed the ring," I gulped, in a voice way weaker and less commanding than my singing one.

Mr. Murdock had been holding up his hands to ward off the flying paper. Now that there was a break in the paper storm, he lowered them to peer at Frank.

Who shrugged again and gave a rueful smile. Charmingly rueful. "Go ahead and search me — if you want," Frank said, his nice tone and manner implying that Mr. Murdock was too smart to bother.

The producer scowled back at me. That was the problem. He liked Frank, and he didn't like me.

I looked at Frank. Those untroubled greens looked back.

And suddenly I knew he didn't have the moonstone, not on him. Even if the security guards tipped him upside down and shook him, it wouldn't fall out. It was somewhere else. He'd already got rid of it.

Frank had outfoxed me.

Mr. Murdock began to splutter some insult about loud girls being troublemakers. "*Wait*," said Jon.

He knelt beside me. His thin, bearded, bespectacled face wasn't nearly as handsome as Frank's. It was ever so much nicer, though.

Something gleamed in Jon's mild brown eyes. Trust. He may not have been sure whether to believe me, but he believed *in* me.

He murmured, "Dinah, you gotta focus. *What is it you know?*"

Gotta focus. Easy for him to say. People were stirring, restless to get out; Mr. Murdock was wheezing, a sure sign he was about to resume his yelling; the cast and crew in the wings were already ripping out fresh script pages to crumple up and lob at him. How could I focus? All this stuff was jumbling up my brain even more than it had been before.

Gotta focus. That's what he and Mr. Paigely had said to me about math. *Just let yourself see it.* In the absence of my pen, I began to chew my lower lip. I remembered the problem of Jane's mother and the pies, and how I'd tried to see through all that stuff about kids staying home and —

All that stuff.

I had to get past the *stuff*.

With an effort I pushed the stuff out of my brain. I plucked at the waterfall of lace that was Cindi's sleeve. "What did Frank do after he grabbed the ring off your finger?" I demanded.

Cindi lifted the lacy sleeve and wept into it. Uh-oh. Soon it would be a real waterfall. "He k-kissed me," she sobbed. "So deceitful! I thought — I thought he *liked* me!"

There was a crashing sound from the audience seats. Hurrying towards us, Mr. Paigely had stumbled against one of the seats.

"Forget the kiss, Cindi," I said, quelling impatience. (Women! The scary thing was, *I* was doomed to turn into one someday. In less than a month I'd have my twelfth birthday.) "The kiss is just *stuff*. Like Jane's pies. Or the things you clean out from your closet, clothes and books and toys that nobody needs anymore, and you leave them all outside in a bag for Big Brothers."

"Huh?" sniffed Cindi, bewildered. But both Jon and Mr. Paigely were regarding me with a funny, fond kind of pride.

"Think about what happened besides the kiss,"

I told Cindi. "Frank had to have done something with the ring. Maybe he swallowed it. Or threw it into the audience — that's what he accused you of. Maybe he tossed it to an accomplice."

"Ridiculous!" barked Frank. He stomped up to his uncle. "How long do we have to listen to this pudgy eardrum-splitter?"

By now Mr. Paigely had reached the stage's edge; he held up a small package of tissues to Cindi. "Allergies," he explained. "I carry tissues everywhere."

"Th-thank you." Cindi blew her nose. "N-no, I don't think Frank had time to throw the ring anywhere. He ran to the side of the stage. Where he is now."

So ... ? He must have passed the ring on to one of those people bunched in the wings. Another member of the cast or crew.

But his accomplice was Beak-Nose, and she wasn't one of them.

Mr. Murdock spluttered out protests — "Shhh!" Jon told him. "Dinah, think. What do you *know*?"

"I know that his accomplice is Beak-Nose Bridey," I said slowly. I shifted to a fresh part of my lower lip to chew. Surveying the people in both of the wings, I saw no one who resembled Violet Bridey.

And yet, what had Angela said about her aunt?

That *she could play any part*.

Curious about what was going on, Cindi stopped weeping. She dropped her hand, clutching one of Mr. Paigely's tissues, which she'd been using to mop at her eyes.

"But where could Mrs. Bridey be?" Jon whispered. He, too, looked around. "This is everyone, Di."

As Cindi let her hand fall, the lacy sleeve made a faint *whish!* against her dress.

Reminding me of the whishing sound I'd heard at every rehearsal.

"It's not quite everyone," I said.

I climbed up on the chair so I could see over the heads of Frank and the cast and crew crammed behind them.

Beyond them, slinking towards the theater's side-door exit, was the stooped, gray-haired cleaning woman.

"THAT'S VIOLET BRIDEY!" I yelled. "SHE HAS THE RING!"

The cleaning woman straightened out of her stoop — and her petiteness. Suddenly tall, she picked up the long folds of her musty navy velvet dress and ran to the exit with gi-normous, unladylike strides.

The security guard who'd laughed heartily at

his own weak joke wasn't as dim-witted as I'd thought. Growling, he ploughed through cast and crew — he shoved some aside so violently they fell backward — and stomped over to the cleaning woman. He grabbed her by one skinny arm before she could scamper out the side door.

"Unhand me, you oaf!" she shrieked in hoity-toity, very un-cleaning-woman-like tones.

She tried squirming free. In the struggle, her stand-on-end gray hair loosened and tumbled to the ground: a wig. Several black teeth, jarred from her mouth, plopped down the navy velvet folds like so many Smarties. *Fake* black teeth.

Her wrinkled skin, or rather not her skin at all, but layers of gray, yellowy makeup, stayed on, except for a thick chunk that smeared against the security guard's jacket sleeve. When the chunk came off, the distinctive nose was at last revealed.

Beak-Nose Bridey grimaced out at us, her eyes wild, her teeth bared in fury, her plans spoiled.

"Got it!" exclaimed the security guard, prying the ring from her clenched, bony fingers. He held it aloft and waved it about. The creamy surface lit up, turned shadowy, combined both light and shadow.

As changeable as the moon, I thought, but a lot more trouble. The nice thing about the moon was it could never be bought, not by Mr. Murdock or anyone else, so it could never be stolen. Way up in the sky there, it belonged to everyone. Whatever mood it was in.

Suddenly, right in my ear, Cindi let out a blood-curdling scream.

"Ow," I winced, rubbing my ear — then I saw what she'd screamed about.

Frank was leaping over the audience seats like a pole vaulter. He was being wily as ever: the aisles were jammed with audience members.

At a wheezed command from Mr. Murdock, the security guards scrambled down after Frank. But they were too burly to leap the way Frank did, lightly and smoothly. Everyone else just gaped, mesmerized by Frank's impressive wide kicks as he sailed over seat back after seat back. His legs swung like windmill blades —

Windmill. I'd been mesmerized, too, but then I thought of the Windmill Café, and Frank, in his Leo guise, shoving me backward into the washroom. To give me "a bit of a scare," he'd chortled nastily.

"STOP HIM, SOMEBODY!" I yelled. There were some ushers and a few audience members at the back of the theater. I aimed my voice at them. "STOP HIM! HE'S THE THIEF!"

Frank cleared the last row of seats. The people

at the back glanced uncertainly at each other.

"COME ON," I bellowed — the problem was, a lot of other people were now making noise as well. The cast was shouting "Scumbag!" "Lowlife!" (and other words I can't really repeat here) at Frank. Mr. Murdock, overcome with excitement, was coughing long, rasping coughs that sounded like the snorting of a horse.

Beak-Nose Bridey was screeching at Frank to be a man and stick by her.

Frank was sprinting towards the double doors that led to the lobby — and escape. From outside the theater, we heard the whine of sirens. Somebody had phoned the police. Would they see Frank before he scooted out onto the busy Granville Street sidewalk and blended in with passersby?

Was it possible Frank would get away?

Then, just as Frank got to the double doors — a man stepped through them, blocking his way.

Jack!

Thank you, Air Canada, I thought. Love those plane delays!

Frank had to stop short to avoid slamming into Jack, who was now edging aside to let him pass.

"JACK, STOP HIM!" I yelled.

Jack looked around, confused by the bright lights and the audience exiting in what was supposed to be the middle of Act I. Confused also by the racket coming at him from all directions.

If there was ever a time to belt my voice out, this was it. Frank's own words of encouragement came back to me: *You can do it if anyone can.*

Okay, Frank. You got it.

"JA-A-A-ACK! Stop him — he's a thief!"

Outblasted, everyone else lapsed into a surprised silence. Well, almost. Beak-Nose kept wailing and the approaching sirens kept whining.

"Hi, kid," Jack greeted me across the rows of seats. "Who'm I supposed to stop?"

Frank was sliding past.

"HIM!" I yelled.

Jack shoved the palm of his hand against Frank's chest. To my alarm, Frank gave Jack one of his charming smile-shrug routines. He murmured something, probably to the effect that this was all some Dinah-mite mistake.

Bewildered, Jack shouted at me, "*This* guy? Who is he?"

Great — now I was making introductions. "Frank!" I yelled back in despair. Even my voice wouldn't be able to belt out a whole long series of explanations.

"Frank!?" Jack clutched Frank by the collar. "You're *Frank?*" He drew back his free hand, fisting it.

I broke into a delighted grin. The "how well do you communicate with your boyfriend?" survey was paying off big-time! Cool or what?

"Take this, buddy!"

And *bam!* Jack punched Frank in the nose, toppling him to the floor.

21.
In the HEADLINES!

"The role of Violet Bridey's life," Jon exclaimed, wiping his forehead with yet another of Mr. Paigely's tissues. "I *thought* the theater wasn't looking as clean as it normally did."

"Her mind obviously wasn't on dustballs," Mother pointed out.

We were sitting backstage with Madge, Jack and Pantelli. Madge was smiling contentedly at Jack, a smug, cat-like smile, in fact, as if she alone had lured him home early from his visit back east.

Of course there was no reason for her to believe otherwise. She didn't know about the boyfriend-communications survey I'd sent Jack on her behalf.

Jack, meanwhile, was giving her a look that was half-glaring, half-adoring. I could see he had some questions for her about the guy he'd just punched — I hoped I wouldn't be present when he got around to asking them. Could be a touch awkward.

The rest of the cast and crew were backstage, too. Everyone was gathered in clumps, chatting excitedly about the dramatic exit that had just occurred, starring Beak-Nose Bridey and Frank.

It was not the type of exit Beak-Nose, with her fierce acting ambitions, would have craved. The police had bustled her and Frank out, followed by a wheezing, spluttering Mr. Murdock, chubby white fist upraised.

"Frank almost got away with his role, too — of the kind, charming friend to Dinah," said Mother, shuddering. She squished me in her approximately hundred-and-first hug of the night. "To think that he locked you in the Windmill Café washroom! And you didn't tell me!"

I was kind of regretting having told her about it now. Somehow I had the feeling I'd be hearing about this for months, even years, to come ...

"He was trying to scare me," I explained. "In his disguise as the mysterious Leo, I mean. Then, I dunno, I *was* going to tell you — till Frank got in the way. He made me think that you and Jon would be mad at me. That you might even pull me out of the show."

I heaved a huge sigh, which got me motherly hug number one hundred and two. "Frank really was devious. He kept tricking me into focusing on the wrong things. Until the end, when I suddenly saw the whole mystery as a math problem, full of information you need — and information you don't, like Jane's pies."

I managed an embarrassed grin at Jon. "I finally clued into the idea of focusing, just like you and Mr. Paigely said. Uh ... Mr. Paigely?"

The substitute teacher never heard me. He and Cindi were too busy gazing at each other over steaming cups of tea.

"This flavor is hazelnut crème, Hugill," Cindi told him, smiling.

Hugill? The other kids in the class better not hear about this.

"Ah, Cindi." Mr. Paigely's happy sigh dispersed hazelnut crème steam around the two of them like a shawl. "There are so many flavors of tea for us to go through together. It could take us years — a lifetime, even."

Frowning at Madge, Jack interrupted. "I have a lifetime's worth of questions for *you*, Ms. Galloway. What did you mean, you found Frank 'attractive and easy to talk to'? What am I, chopped liver?"

Madge's cat-like smile faded. She stared at him.

"Huh? I've never exchanged so much as two words with Frank."

They regarded each other in bewilderment for a moment longer — then, slowly, they turned to me ...

The next morning at school, Mr. Paigely didn't even try to get our class to do regular work. He just passed around copies of the *Vancouver Sun*, which was crammed with stories about the exciting events at the theater. "Let's have a current events period," he suggested — and then burrowed into his copy of the *Sun*, forgetting about us.

BETTER THAN ANY PLAY! blared the front page in huge, thick black letters. Also hugely featured: a photo of Mr. Murdock at his most enraged, his flabby white fist upraised and his mouth open cavernously wide in mid-yell. I peered into it, half-expecting to see stalactites forming.

There was only one thing that took away from the fun of reading about Beak-Nose and Frank and — ahem! — my cleverness in figuring out their plan. I was pretty sure the photo of Mr. Murdock had been taken when he was yelling at me, when he'd been mad at me for interrupting the show.

I had the uncomfortable feeling Mr. Murdock was still mad at me. Last night, as the police had gone around questioning everyone, Mr. Murdock kept grumbling about "loud" people and their unsettling effect on his nerves.

So unfair. "What happened was Beak-Nose's and Frank's fault, not mine," I'd muttered to Jon.

"But Frank's his nephew," Jon had reminded me. "It'll take a while for the truth to sink in, that a member of his own family was trying to steal from him."

I doubted anything could sink into that flushed, roly-poly figure. Nope. The guy just didn't like me. He'd wanted a pure, operatic voice for his play, like Angela Bridey's.

Now, with a sigh, I settled down to read more of the stories.

First off, the matter of the Livingston Theater's cleaning woman. It was Frank, using his influence as Mr. Murdock's nephew, who'd fired the former cleaning woman and, surprise, surprise, hired a heavily costumed Beak-Nose to replace her, under an assumed name.

It turned out that Frank and Beak-Nose had met while auditioning for a play. Neither had got a part in it, but the stage had certainly been set for romance.

And for plotting.

Both had ambitions to move to New York.

Neither felt appreciated: Frank by his uncle, Beak-Nose by the local theater community. They planned to ransom the moonstone back to Mr. Murdock. Then, unsavory profits in hand, they intended to act, or at least audition, on Broadway.

We'll walk along Broadway, Frank had sung to me the night he, Cindi, Mother, Jon and I went out for sushi. He'd meant it more seriously than I realized — I thought he'd been teasing me about my chances of becoming a star.

Maybe he had been, partly. I flipped to an inside page, where Frank, in a promotional photo as Miss Verinder's fiancé, grinned charmingly out at me. In spite of everything, I found myself grinning back at him. I remembered how Frank had praised my singing, and how pleased I'd felt.

That, at least, hadn't been phony: he'd meant what he said. Even though — my grin turned into a grimace — he'd also been setting me, or rather my voice, up as a cover for Cindi's screams when he grabbed the ring.

I chewed my pen end. My agent, Mr. Wellman, had once asked me if I could accept that people could be imperfect, neither totally good nor totally bad. That was a concept I was still struggling with.

I read on. Frank's parents had been killed in a plane crash when he was five. His uncle had taken care of him after that. "I sent him to the best boarding schools and camps," Mr. Murdock had wept to reporters. "I gave the kid everything."

"Hmm. Everything except himself," commented Ms. Chen over my shoulder, making me jump.

The principal had glided up in that annoying silent way principals have. She said, "Instead, Mr. Murdock lavished all his love on his gems, the moonstone most of all. Maybe, by trying to steal the moonstone, Frank was trying to steal some of the love he himself had never got from his uncle."

"Heav-*eeee*," breathed Pantelli, his brown eyes round with awe.

Ms. Chen looked rather pleased — until she noticed he was reading an article on city bylaws protecting trees and not listening to her at all.

"Well," she said acidly, "*you* must have a contribution to make to this discussion, Dinah. After all, you unmasked the thieves."

"I always have a contribution to discussions," I assured her.

Just then the much-chewed end of the pen came off in my mouth. I wanted to tell Ms. Chen about Frank disguising himself as Leo and being a bully to me in the Windmill Café, and how this almost made it impossible for me to feel sorry for him, but not completely.

Instead, with the pen end on my tongue, all I could say was, "Ogfmltch."

The principal scrutinized me. "I beg your pardon, Dinah? Are you part of this discussion or not? Please do give us your contribution."

I opened my mouth. The pen end tumbled out onto my desk.

"I ... see," Ms. Chen said, very coldly. "Mr. Paigely!" she called, with a sharp clapping of her hands. *Not* the applause kind of clapping.

Mr. Paigely looked up in confusion from his copy of the *Sun*. He wore a silly, rather adoring kind of expression. Though I wasn't close enough to see, I bet he'd been reading the feature article on Cindi, titled A SCREAMINGLY GOOD ACTRESS.

"I beg your — ? Oh, it's you, Ms. Chen." Mr. Paigely got up too quickly, knocking the various sections of the *Sun* off all sides of his desk.

"I think it may be time to get some work done, Mr. Paigely," Ms. Chen snapped as she exited the classroom.

22.
Dinah versus the butterflies

Ms. Chen wasn't the only one unamused by the reading of newspapers.

"WHAT'S THIS?" Mr. Murdock bellowed, waving the *Sun* around at the *Moonstone* cast and crew. "Did you see this? 'Better than any play!' it says. Who's gonna take my production seriously after this? They're gonna want more cops an' robbers!"

"No, no," Jon soothed the temperamental producer, who'd worked himself into an unbecoming beet color. And into a series of explosive wheezes. "This has been great publicity, sir. Look, the theater's packed!"

He lifted the curtain. Mr. Murdock, and those of us close by him, peeked out. It was true. The place resembled the inside of a sardine can.

Mr. Murdock had been wiping at his forehead with a handkerchief the size of a small tablecloth; now he dabbed at his eyes with it. "They're here because they've read about my nephew. They've caught a whiff of scandal and they've descended — oh, the vultures!" he wept. "They're not here for *art*."

I studied Mr. Murdock curiously. It had never occurred to me that this crude fat man could care about art. He'd only seemed interested in bragging about his famous moonstone — now back under strict guard, by the way, at his jewelry store — and in palming off as many as possible of those cheap imitation moonstones for sale in the lobby.

"Dreadful!" sobbed Mr. Murdock. Then he caught sight of me ogling him. "You. The loud girl. What have you to say for yourself, missy?"

"A lot," I assured him. It was true: being stuck for words had never been my problem. "Let's see." I tapped my fingertips against my chin. When it came to topics, there was so *much* to choose from. "Oh yeah. I did okay in a math test today. There was another one of those problems, this time about a boy named Edward who had to buy football tickets for his twelve friends and their fathers. Except that some of his buddies wanted to bring brothers along, too. Only Edward wasn't sure how many."

A bell tinkled: five minutes till curtain went up. I plunged on, aware of Jon making those slicing signs across his throat with his forefinger, "I realized that I had to focus, just like Jon and Mr. Paigely kept telling me to. See, before I'd have only thought about Edward and what a doofus he was."

I grinned at Mr. Murdock, prepared to like him even though he *was* bad-humored.

And I would have kept chatting, in spite of Jon's ever-more-frantic slicing motions, because there was so very much that was interesting to talk about. Life was like one of those calendars where you flip up a piece of cardboard for each day and find a treat underneath. Okay, so there were tricks as well as treats, as I'd discovered in this season of Halloween and moonstones, but there was never *nothing*, if you know what I mean.

The producer crushed his flabby white hands over his ears. "YOU," he steamed. "YOU, MISSY, ARE TOO LOUD AND TOO MUCH!"

He stomped off, unfortunately treading on Cindi's slippered feet. She let loose one of her most impressive screams.

On the other side of the curtain, the audience assumed the scream was the start of the play. They clapped, cheered and whistled.

The butterflies were back. They weren't just *fluttering* in my stomach. They were marching around in battalions.

"I can't go onstage," I told Jon. "Maybe you

could do some fast scene rewrites and eliminate the Coretta Cuff character altogether."

"That's problematic."

"Yeah? Why?"

"You make your entrance in two minutes."

It was the "Blue Moon" number. Cindi was singing her part; the spotlight would veer to the middle of the stage, currently dark, where I would belt out my part. My full part this time, with no screams or thieves to interrupt the proceedings.

My agent, Mr. Wellman, had said anxiously to me backstage, "Promise me, tonight no thief-catching. It's not often a singer gets another chance at a career launch. In fact, this may be a first in the history of theater."

Then he'd sighed. "So *many* things are firsts with you, Dinah Galloway."

Talk about pressure — again.

Now, behind me, the young man who'd been Frank's understudy and was taking over his role as of this performance was busy throwing up. "Sorry. First-evening jitters," he kept apologizing. "I'll be fine once I get onstage. Oops, 'scuse me ... " — and then he'd heave again.

I gulped. "My sentiments exactly," I told Jon. "Mr. Murdock doesn't like my singing — and he's the *producer*."

"I hope that's not my box of spare scripts you're throwing up into," Jon admonished the young man.

"Aw, no, Henry. It *is*."

Jon turned back to me and squeezed my hand. "Listen, kid. Your singing reaches everyone because you put your heart into it. And you've got a big, big heart. A strange mind, but a big heart."

I regarded him thoughtfully. Just for that instant he wasn't my boss anymore, but my friend, and the person who liked my mother a lot. I managed a weak, but pleased, smile.

Then Jon put on his businesslike director's expression again — though with a bit of a twinkle visible behind his glasses. "About Murdy. Listen. If he says he doesn't like your voice, it's because you're reaching *him*, too. Your singing is reminding him somehow of — I dunno, the plump, young Murdy who ... maybe ... used to romp through fields, collecting daisies instead of gemstones. A time, anyhow, when he was much happier than now, except that he doesn't want to admit it."

I giggled at the thought of Mr. Murdock "romping." Some of the butterflies in my stomach went away. I thought of the things Dad, and now Jon, had told me about my singing, and more of the butterflies left. I took a huge breath. Maybe they'd flown off to where they belonged — to fields like the ones Jon had described.

Frank's understudy lifted his head from the box of spare manuscripts he was barfing into. "*I* could use one of your rah-rah pep talks," he informed Jon rather sulkily.

Cindi was almost finished her part of "Blue Moon." The spotlight was going to swing to my part of the stage, and I had to be there.

"Wait," I said to Jon, as he began trying to soothe Frank's understudy out of throwing up anymore. I had a last, teeny worry. "Mr. Murdock thinks I sing too loud. What should I do?"

Jon looked at me in his solemn director's way. Then he grinned ever so slightly. A proud grin — proud of *me*. "Sing louder," he said.

I grinned, too. I tiptoed onstage, stuffing my glasses in a pocket of the fluffy crinoline dress I had to wear. Jon was right. I would just keep on singing, and loudly, because that was me. It was the gift I had, it was what I loved and it was what I did.

Cindi finished. The spotlight slid off her, towards me. I'd better stuff this grin away as well, since Coretta was supposed to be feeling sad in this scene.

Wiped from my face, the grin must've gone to my heart. As the spotlight covered me, I felt glad, really gi-normously glad, to be onstage. Butterflies belonged in fields. I belonged here.

Melanie Jackson wrote her first mystery story at age seven and hasn't stopped since. She isn't sure why she likes mysteries so much, except that maybe it's part of being interested in life and its possibilities. Like, what *is* just around the next corner? Melanie used to be a freelance writer and editor until Dinah came along and bossily demanded all her creative attention. These days Melanie and her cat, Matthew, get up very early in the morning - *very* early - to work on Dinah's adventures before Melanie heads off to her day job at an education organization.

Melanie lives in Dinah's neighborhood, on Vancouver's East Side, with — besides the cat — her husband, Bart and daughter, Sarah-Nelle. Melanie isn't sure who inspired Dinah. Sometimes she thinks Dinah has the personality she herself would *like* to have, if she had the nerve. Dinah definitely has the voice Melanie always wanted. Melanie loves listening to the music of belter-outers such as Judy Garland and Bessie Smith, though her favorite song of all time is performed by Louis Armstrong. You guessed it. The title is ... *Dinah*.